THE LONE RANGER:
VENDETTA

by

Howard Hopkins

visit us on the web at:
www.moonstonebooks.com

1

Two weeks ago…
#

The shovel plunging into the hardpack made a sound like a Bowie knife grating against bone. The figure wielding the implement grunted, stamped a booted heel atop the shovel's edge, driving it deeper into the ground. The first thrust was always the most difficult, the earth baked damn near as hard as rock in the small canyon. The next came easier, the ground below already having been disturbed long ago when the grave was dug.

The figure continued to dig, thrusting the shovel into the earth again and again; muscles weary after five previous exhumations, but will unrelenting. For vengeance, once poisoning the mind and coursing through the veins, was a powerful drug.

The copper sun beat down on the figure, who wore a grime-coated duster, worn boots and denim trousers, with unmerciful intensity. Heavy cattleman's gloves protected smallish hands from blisters, and the figure appeared built along the lines of a teenaged boy, with straight hips and a loose denim shirt. Sweat soaked great patches of the shirt beneath the arms and chest. A low-pulled battered hat shadowed the figure's face, and errant strands of dirty blonde hair, cut short, protruded around the ears.

The figure continued digging as the sun rose higher, burning from a sapphire sky; long shadows within the canyon dissolved and waves of heat rippled from the dusty ground, distorting the scrub-peppered hills making up the horizon. Pausing, the figure's gaze swung to the walls of the canyon, a place called Bryant's Gap, a place of infamy, a place of violent death. For an instant, it was as if the figure could hear the thundering echoes of hoof beats and gunshots, the gasps of dying men and laughter and whoops of outlaws cascading in demonic rhythm from the past.

A whispered laugh trickled from the figure's parched throat. With renewed effort, the figure returned to the task at hand.

The deeper the hole became, the more hate swelled within the figure's heart. For only dirt and more dirt came from the grave, the last of six the figure had exhumed. When at last the hole was deep enough, the figure stepped back and hurled the shovel into a small patch of brush that grew from the rock-strewn canyon floor at the base of a precarious trail leading up to the left ridge.

"Christ on a crutch…" the figure whispered, voice lacking enough tone to identify it clearly as male or female, young or old.

The figure stepped back, surveying the six opened graves, fury running like quicksilver through its veins. Beside each the first five graves lay the rotting corpse of a man, remains now little more than skeletons with dried pieces of flesh and scraps of clothing clinging to gray bone. Five men. Five Texas Rangers. Murdered under a hail of lead from an outlaw named Butch

Cavendish and his gang, who had waited in ambush that day long ago.

"Jim Bates…" the figure whispered, the words dissolving on a scorching breeze hushing through the canyon. "Sam Cooper…" The figure stepped sideways to the next graves, hidden ice-green eyes intent on the dirt-caked, decomposed Rangers. "Jack Stacy…Joe Brandt…"

The figure paused again; tongue running over dry chapped lips. "Captain Dan Reid…"

A moment drifted by. A buzzard circled high above. The ghosts of the past seemed to cry on the stifling breeze.

The figure returned to the last grave, stood for dragging heartbeats peering into its empty maw.

"And you…where are you, young Reid?" The figure's voice climbed with rising anger. Husky and deep, it sounded almost boyish, despite the figure's 32 years. As the figure knelt before the grave, the folds of its denim shirt parted where a button had popped off during the digging and sunlight penetrated the opening to reveal a dirt-smudged glimpse of breast beneath.

A laugh trickled from shadowed lips, the tone higher now, echoing through the canyon, the sound more distinct, feminine.

"You should have died that day with the rest, Masked Man." The figure stood, head lifting, sunlight striking a woman's boyish, dust-dirtied features. "I reckon I'll see about remedying that."

She turned, walked toward a horse tethered to the branch of a scrub brush ten feet distant. She would let the prairie wolves attend to the Rangers' bones, while

3

she attended to those of the living.

The empty grave, she vowed…would not remain empty for long.

The nightmare came in blood and amber. The sun, like enflamed topaz, blazed down on the six riders holding a steady gait as they entered Bryant's Gap. Rangers. Texas Rangers. Men with muscles as hardened as gunmetal and nerves as strong as iron. Men with wills as shining as silver.

Yet apprehension prickled through the hairs on the back of the young Ranger's neck who held to the front beside a man a few years older than he, a sixth sense that warned him something was wrong, dead wrong, though he could not determine what.

His six-foot-one frame stiffened in the saddle and his square chin came forward a hair, as if in defiance of the unease swarming through his being. His gaze lifted, blue eyes searching the ridge above the gnarled canyon walls to either side of the Rangers who rode single-file, with the exception of himself and his brother, for any signs of an ambush: sunlight glinting off the metal of a rifle or Smith & Wesson hand gun, the stirring of brush that grew in sporadic patches along the ridge, a glimpse of a bushwhacker slipping from boulder to boulder.

Nothing.

And yet…

Their mission belied the calm, but strengthened the vague dread in his nerves. Capture or kill the Blood

Creek Gang, a gang led by a man with no compassion, and no trace of mercy when it came to the victims who'd perished under his lead. Robbery, murder, rape. This man was responsible for all of those, and more. If ever the Devil walked in the form of man…this outlaw was it.

An easy laugh came from the man wearing the black vest beside him, his brother, Dan, a man a few years his senior, a hundred his experience. At least as far as he saw it. He worshiped Captain Dan Reid, as did many of the Rangers under his command. Wished he could someday grow into half the man his brother had become. For if Dan Reid was gold, the younger Reid would settle for silver.

"What's got your gizzard, kid?" Dan Reid asked, glancing his way, the glint of ever-present humor and compassion strong in his gray eyes. "You look like you've seen a ghost."

The younger Reid gazed his brother's away. For a moment, his brother's face vanished, flesh melting away and leaving a weathered grinning death's head. A gasp caught in his throat and his gloved hands tightened on the big chestnut's reins until his fingers pained and his forearms ached. As blood began steaming down the skull, every muscle in his body tightened. He swore his heart stopped beating.

"What is it, son?" Dan Reid asked, concern gripping his voice.

"I…" The younger Ranger shook his head, and the bleeding skull disappeared, replaced by the worried features of his kin.

"Speak up, boy! You ill? For the last couple hours

you've been looking as pale as a bargal who just discovered all the fellas moved out of town."

"Cavendish…" he whispered through teeth a fraction apart.

Dan Reid frowned, nodded slightly. The lines webbing from his eyes deepened and his brow knotted. "He's a bastard, shore enough. But we'll get him. No need to be afeared of him. He's just a man and all men bleed."

The younger Reid swallowed at the fear balling in his throat, trying to force his unsubstantiated dread away. After all, they had every advantage, didn't they? Cavendish and his gang did not know they were on their trail, did not know the guide named Collins scouting ahead had gotten a lead on their hideout. The element of surprise and experience was on their side.

"Ain't afraid to admit I'm scared, Dan. Something doesn't *feel* right." He swiped at the dust, kicked up from the horses' hoofs, that coated his brow, the beads of sweat there trickling and carrying it into his eyes, making them sting.

His brother blew out a heavy sigh, shifted in the saddle. "Cavendish don't know we're comin', son. He's always had the jump on those poor souls he's killed, but things are different this time…" Dan Reid paused, unspoken thoughts crossing his face. "Just the same…my wife and son are coming from back East. Anything happens to me…promise you'll see they're taken of. Askin' you as kin…and as a friend. We got that silver mine we've been plannin' on workin'…give my share to them."

The younger Reid nodded, the request doing noth-

7

ing to ease the tension in his frame. "This man, Collins…you trust him completely?"

Dan Reid shrugged, but it came without complete conviction. "He's known in the area, got a good reputation. His information has all checked out accurate. I reckon he's trustworthy…though I'm keepin' my eyes open. Seen no signs of anything suspicious to this point."

"Don't like the way he's ridin' ahead so much. Almost like he's waiting on something."

A flash of concern on Dan Reid's features told the younger Ranger the same thought had crossed his brother's mind more than once.

"Cavendish is a ballsy sonofabitch, ain't no denyin' that. But he ain't about to attack a group of Texas Rangers…"

With those words, the younger Ranger's nightmare began in earnest.

"Look," the younger Ranger said, jutting an arm straight out, gloved finger pointing.

Up ahead a few hundred yards, a man had sat his horse, was peering back at them. Even from the distance the smile on his face was plain.

"Collins…" Dan Reid muttered. "What the hell?"

A shout rang out from one of the Rangers behind them. The younger Reid's head swiveled, and his gaze jerked upward to where the Ranger who had uttered the cry was pointing, but it was too late.

Thunder boomed from the walls of Bryant's Gap. The thunder of gunshots. Gunshots accompanied by leaden rain.

"Jesus!" Dan Reid muttered and was off his horse

in a heartbeat, running for the shelter of a small boulder ten feet away. "Christ, son, get the hell down!" The snapping words, flung back over a shoulder, shook the younger Reid from momentary inaction. But they didn't come in time. A piercing burning pain stabbed his left shoulder as a bullet punched through cloth and flesh. He uttered a clipped cry, the impact driving him sideways and nearly from the saddle. He managed to grab the horn with his right hand, keep himself from being blasted free of his mount. His boot tangled in the stirrup and driven half by panic he pulled at it as the horse, spooked by the clamoring shots, suddenly reared and beat the air with its hoofs. A frightened neigh ululated through the morning as the horse came down again, hoofs slamming against the hardpack with a jolt that traveled throughout his entire body and clacked his teeth together.

He uttered a short yell, trying to steady the animal, but it was useless. The chestnut's front legs came off the ground again, and his hand jerked free of its hold. He went down, twisting; boot caught half in the stirrup. The beast's hoofs hit ground, and the animal thrust forward, as more shots filled the morning.

The animal dragged him ten feet before his boot came loose of the stirrup. The horse bolted, its cries pitiful and frightened, and a glimpse told him it had been hit in the flank, nearly the only thing that would send that well-trained creature into such a headlong gallop.

Everything around him seemed to slow, as if time somehow dragged, each second becoming a tortured moment. He was barely conscious of himself rising from the ground, his legs driving him toward where his brother had headed.

About him thunder crashed from the canyon walls and hammered against his eardrums. Horses reared, panicked bleats slicing through the thunder. The world was an amber and blood painting, one stroked with death and terror.

He made it to the rocks along the canyon's base, whirled, hand sweeping for the Colt Army Model 1860 at his hip. Shots came from his gun, as if they were triggered by someone else, not him. His brother fired beside him, blood spattered on his fingers, and the younger Reid realized his kin had been wounded somewhere as well.

Other Rangers died quickly. One, Jim Bates, was blasted out of his saddle, seemed to hang momentarily in the air before slamming to the hardpack, unmoving. Another, Sam Cooper, went down halfway to a boulder, dead finger still reflexively triggering shots until the weapon's recoil tore it from his grip.

Jack Stacy and Joe Brandt reached meager shelter, but the rain of lead was too much for them. From the right rim of the canyon it blazed down, from men hidden behind brush and boulders, firing shot after shot. Bullets tore into both men, and their guns went silent.

"Jesus, son, we're done for!" Dan Reid shouted, panic in his voice for the first time the younger Reid could recall. "I love ya, son. Run!"

With those words Captain Dan Reid came from his shelter, guns raised, blazing, triggering shot after shot.

"Nooo!" the younger Reid screamed, knowing his

10

brother was trying to give him a chance, however slim, of escape by sacrificing his own life.

As if in response, the storm of lead grew louder, more insistent. The younger Reid came up, seeking to back up his brother. But Captain Dan Reid staggered as a bullet punched into his chest, jolting his body about like a marionette suddenly without strings. Blood sprayed and holes stitched a line across his shirt. Then his face disappeared in a gruesome pulp of scarlet, and his body crumpled.

Blood, flesh and chips of bone splattered the younger Ranger and he was only conscious of himself screaming over and over: "Cavendish! I'll kill you! You hear me? *I'll kill you!*" His Colt came up, but the hammer fell with an empty clack.

And bullets found him. Their impact drove him back, back. He slammed against the canyon wall. The gun flew from his grip, landed on the hardpack. A glance downward told him he had been hit multiple times. Strangely, no pain came with the wounds, and in fact he felt nothing throughout his body. His legs buckled and he went forward, crashed into the ground face first.

#

A scream formed deep within the Lone Ranger's throat as he jolted awake, but he managed to choke it off before it fled into the night. The white hat covering his eyes while he slept flew to the ground. His heart pounded and, sitting up on the heavy blanket on the cool ground, he put his head in his hands, trying to shake off the remnants of the nightmare.

Nightmare? Yes. And, no. A blood-memory, for

11

while the events of that fateful day did indeed haunt his dreams, they had been all too real. His brother and four other men had perished that day, the result of a trap set by a madman, and the guilt of having lived through it, having been the sole survivor, was something that would ride with him the rest of his born days.

His face came from his hands, blue eyes moist with stinging loss and grief behind the black half-mask he'd made from his brother's vest.

"The nightmare again, Kemosabe?" came the deep voice of a man standing beyond the fire, at the edge of the camp. The man wore buckskins and a band about his forehead, had his back to the man the West knew only as the Lone Ranger.

For a moment the Masked Man didn't answer as his mind struggled to make sense of that day. But the answer always came back the same: it made no sense; wanton hate and murder never did. Men like Butch Cavendish made no sense; they never would.

The gentle nickering of a great white horse tethered the branch of a cottonwood at the south edge of the camp brought him from his thoughts. A second mount, a pinto, was tethered near the white stallion.

The fire crackled and popped and the smoky musk of burning branches scented the night air.

"Yes," the Ranger said at last. "They've gotten worse, more frequent the closer we get to Bryant's Gap."

The Lone Ranger came to his feet, leaving his brace of ivory-handled Peacemaker .45s holstered in his gunbelt next to the blanket. From habit and caution, his gaze swept over his surroundings, but the danger

12

was minimal for the time being. No one knew they were here and any threat from stray Apache was negated by the fact the band did not stalk at night, save under an Apache moon, fearing if killed their souls would forever wander in darkness on the other side. His gaze lifted briefly to the fingernail moon above, then returned to the man standing peering out into the night.

Somewhere an owl hooted, the sound mournful. A prairie wolf's lonesome howl punctuated the sentiment. A breeze jostled the flames and blown sand made scratching sounds along the ground.

"Perhaps you should not return to Bryant's Gap, Kemosabe," the man said. "Perhaps the memories are too…"

"Painful?" The Lone Ranger shook his head. "It's been years, Tonto. Butch Cavendish is gone and my brother and those men can rest in peace."

The Lone Ranger stepped up beside the man, who didn't turn, merely folded his arms across his buckskin-clad chest. Strands of long black hair stirred under another vapid breeze. His deep reddish-brown features remained emotionless, though something played behind his dark eyes.

"Someone knows, Kemosabe." Tonto's voice came as if he were utterly convinced of the fact.

The Lone Ranger nodded, a prickle of apprehension running through his nerves—the same uneasy feeling he'd experienced the day of the ambush in Bryant's Gap. It was vague, indefinable, but it was there.

"I'm inclined to agree," he said. "But knows what? And who knows?"

"Trace Cooper sent that telegram to young Reid.

13

He asked specifically for the Lone Ranger."

The same thing troubled the Lone Ranger. That contact had been made through his nephew and had named the Masked Man…that was worrisome. It provided a link to a man the West believed dead, murdered with five other Rangers. There were those in the towns near Bryant's Gap who had known the Reids, remembered the massacre. Had one of them put the pieces together? But how? That should have been impossible. He and Tonto had taken great pains to leave no pieces, no trail.

And yet…

"Sam Cooper's son…" the Lone Ranger muttered with the feeling of someone walking across his grave. "He was a bit younger than I when I met him. He might recognize me if he saw me without the mask, but I haven't been back to Coopersville since that day and we've not crossed trails."

Tonto gazed at the Masked Man, a trace of a smile on his lips. "Men see through masks everyday, Kemosabe. He had reason to send that telegram to young Dan…"

"You're right, of course." The Lone Ranger paused. "And Trace Cooper wouldn't have asked us to come if there weren't a good reason."

"Perhaps it is a trap. Perhaps he intends to expose you."

The Lone Ranger considered it, then shook his head. "If he wanted to do that he would have done so by now. He could have sold the story to Buntline or one of his type, or even a legitimate paperman. No, there's some other reason. His father was a fine Ranger; more

14

than that, he was a fine human being. The few times I met Trace he seemed like an apple off the same tree."

Tonto frowned, looked back out into the night, a trace of melancholy on his face. "I don't like this feeling, Kemosabe. I have not felt it since the day we tracked down Cavendish."

The Ranger remained silent, unable to dispute his friend's notions. Because he felt the same way, and had not been able to shake the feeling since Dan handed him the telegram. Something was wrong. Dead wrong. And somehow it related to that day at Bryant's Gap. They'd reach Coopersville sometime tomorrow. He needed rest, but knew sleep would prove elusive for the remainder of this night. Memories were too close, to acute, too painful.

He peered at his friend and Tonto seemed lost in some world within his mind again, though he wasn't quite sure why the Indian had been that way the past few days.

"What do you see out there, Tonto? In the night…" The Ranger's gaze swept to the sky, its silver-chip stars cold sparks on black velvet.

"I see ghosts, Kemosabe."

"Ghosts?"

"The Ghosts of the Bodéwadmi, the keepers of the fire. They ride with frozen thunder across the black sky forest, the way they once rode the trails and plains. Proud. Free. The world closed in on them and now they are nearly gone. I feel their isolation, their separation from the soil and the lands. They scream their silent pleas to Kichimanido."

The Lone Ranger nodded, and a wave of grief

15

washed over him. Grief and loneliness. The loss of what was, what had been and never would be again. He had lost all that meant anything to him at Bryant's Gap; it had been torn from him by one man. He had lost his identity, to adopt one unknown, perhaps until now, and with that came the very isolation Tonto felt of his own people.

"We have what we have now, Tonto," he said, knowing within his soul with absolute certainty their mission was true and just and necessary.

"I do not wish to lose that, Kemosabe. This time…is different."

Tonto was right. The immediate future would either justify the lives they had chosen, to aide those who needed it, deliver justice to those who deserved it—or it would shatter them and cost their very lives.

3

Nine days ago…
#

The plan was ready, and that excited her. This morning there would be blood, and that excited her even more. She could almost smell the bitter copper in the musty interior of the general store.

It had taken little effort to break into the place. The lock was a simple matter for her; she'd learned long ago to pick all but the most complicated with a twisted length of metal she kept in the pocket of her duster.

She eased the door shut behind her. The hour was early, and few folks were out and about on the wide rutted main street of Coopersville. Those who were paid her little mind, focused on whatever business they intended. Most were headed for the café and the presence of one boyish-looking woman in a low-pulled hat loitering outside the general store had not warranted their attention. Later, when asked to describe anyone who had been near the building they would not be able to do so.

There was the marshal, however, and she would take care of him soon enough, but he was not an early riser. She had learned that much from the three days she'd spent watching the store, its owner and the lawdog. She was nothing if not thorough, and she'd been planning her revenge for a long spell.

Once inside, she stood stock still for a few moments, gaze scanning the rows of canned goods, sacks of flour piled on the worn floorboards, barrels of various goods and shelves stacked with colored bottles of powders, preserves and elixirs. How common. What made a man retire from a life of law for something so plebian? It puzzled her. She would never be able to live such a tedious life. She needed the constant threat of being caught, or killed. She could never be some fancy man or cowboy's wife. It made the blood stagnant, while hers burned hot with vengeance.

She spat, then ground the saliva into the floorboard beneath her boottoe.

Early morning sunlight arced through the grime-coated front window, dust pirouetting within the shaft. Shadows still stretched from shelves and the counter flanking the north wall and fell in jagged slices across the floor, but would soon vanish as the day brightened. Too bad. She liked shadows. Her soul was bathed in them.

She stepped deeper into the store, selected a hard-backed chair opposite the counter and sat. It was Tom Sanders' habit to come in the back way, go straight to that counter. She knew his routine as well as she knew the marshal's.

With a humorless whispered laugh she edged the Smith & Wesson at her waist from its holster and sighted down the barrel at the counter. Not that it was necessary; she rarely missed. But the motion pleased her. She checked the chambers, made sure they were full, then shoved the weapon back into its holster.

Threads, she thought. Threads to a dead man who wasn't really a dead man. No one had put it together, as far as she knew, but she was far smarter than the ordinary owlhoot.

Butch had always told her that.

He was right.

She *was* smarter. Deadlier, too, and more vicious. Facts the Masked Man would soon discover.

The whispered laugh came again and the imagined scent of blood grew stronger in her senses. She'd planned; she'd waited. And now it was time.

"Reid…" Her voice came low, laced with spite. "You fooled them all…but not me."

A sound from the back of the store captured her attention. Her gazed shifted back to the counter. More sounds came, noises of someone rummaging around in the back. One minute passed. Two. Impatience began to crawl through her nerves like fireants.

An older man with iron hair and side whiskers came from the doorway behind the counter leading to the back room, carrying a metal cashbox. That pleased her. Killing was always better when there was money involved.

She watched the man as he placed the box beneath the counter, then scribbled something with a stub of a pencil on a scrap of paper. That he didn't see her was obvious. That pleased her as well.

"Your name's Sanders…" she said and the older man started, letting out a small gasp. He looked like a spider, she thought. His limbs were bony and long, yet his belly strained the lower buttons of his heavy shirt.

He peered at her through wire-rimmed spectacles that made his watery eyes look unnaturally large, squinting to see into the shadows engulfing the chair that was angled just beyond the shaft of light from the window.

"Who are you?" he asked, voice unsteady, unsure of the threat. "What are you doing in here? I'm not open for business yet." He fought to control his voice by speaking a little too loud, but failed.

My, how the mighty had fallen. That results of a life without zest, she thought. Once the hunter, now the hunted.

"I'm aware of that," she said, standing, then stepping into the light so he could see her. The hat brim cast a shadow over her features, but her sex was plain. "The kind of business I got for you ain't for regular hours."

His eyes narrowed further. "You're a girl…"

"Aware of that, too."

"What do you want? How did you get in here?" His blue-veined hands with parchmentlike skin flattened on the countertop, and he leaned forward slightly, as if that were supposed to intimidate her into telling him what he wanted to know. That was more like it. A spark of the man he used to be. But a pitiful spark, one easily snuffed. This man had been strong, once, used to getting answers to his questions. He had been a Ranger. But the years and his dreary life had not been kind to him. If she had even a lick of compassion, she might have felt sorry for him. But she did not. No compassion, no mercy. Some even claimed, no soul.

"You knew the Reids?" she said, ignoring his questions, showing him his days of intimidation were past.

"The Reids?" His face softened and she could see the name brought fond memories. Good. That was exactly what she'd hoped for.

"They were Rangers," she said, taking a step closer to the counter—but not too close.

"I know they were. Worked with Captain Dan a short spell. He was like a son to me and Martha, him and his younger brother. Shared many a meal together. But the Reids are all gone now."

"Are they?" She paused, a thin smile coming to her lips.

The man nodded. "Killed over to Bryant's Gap, long time ago."

"Martha?" she said, ignoring his words. Was there another close to Reid she could use?

"My wife." The older man's voice dropped to nearly a whisper and pain bled into his tone. "She's gone, too, near five years."

She peered at him, expressionless. "You must be very lonely without her…"

He nodded. "I am. Miss her everyday."

"I know loneliness," she said. "Had someone taken from me…"

The older man scratched his head. "Sorry to hear that, miss. But you ain't told me what you're doin' in my store. And what do the Reids have to do with it? They're gone even longer than Martha. You a friend of theirs?"

"Yes…gone." She smiled, a snake of a thing. "Would you like to see her again? Your wife, I mean. Would you like to be with her?"

His brow furrowed. He peered at her as if she were

21

insane, and she reckoned she couldn't hold that against him.

"Give anything. But it ain't possible."

"It's possible…" Thunder punctuated her words. For in a blur, her hand swept to the Smith & Wesson and drew it from the holster. The gun came up in a fraction of a heartbeat and flame and blue smoke erupted from its barrel.

The older man flew backward as lead punched into his chest. He slammed into the wall beside the door, seemed suspended there for dragging moments. He looked down at the blood orchid now on his shirt, disbelief on his face. Then his legs buckled and his eyelids fluttered, and he slid downward, leaving a streak of blood on the wall from where the bullet had exited his back.

He was dead before he hit the floor.

She holstered the gun, the crash of the shot still ringing in her ears. Her hand went to a pocket of her duster, came back out.

She peered at the object in her hand; light from the window glinted from it. A bullet. A copper bullet. Copper reminded her of blood.

With a satisfied laugh, she tossed the bullet over the counter, near the body. It made a hollow sound clattering on the floorboards.

"And so it begins…"

The shot would draw attention soon. She needed to leave. Going around the counter, she stepped over the dead man and grabbed the cashbox. Tucking it beneath her arm, she glanced at the shop owner, then slipped out the back.

He was dead before he hit the floor.

4

The ranch house on the outskirts of Coopersville was a sprawling Hacienda style adobe with walls two feet thick, swiped with *jaspe* tinted red. The heavy front door would have been suitable for a fortress and deep set windows were framed with wood painted blue. Hand-peeled cedar beams overhung the roof and a veranda ran the length of the front. Trimmed grounds gave way to gently rolling hills and grassy swales.

The Lone Ranger and Tonto approached the structure from the east, and the Masked Man drew his great white horse to a halt a hundred yards from the place.

"This belongs to young Cooper?" Tonto asked after reining up beside the Ranger.

The Masked Man nodded, his gaze sweeping the grounds for any signs of life. He noticed a number of outbuildings: an icehouse and storage shed, bunkhouse and barn, smokehouse and springhouse. It was a small spread as far as Texas ranches went, but there should have been activity, and he saw no movement whatsoever. At the very least, smoke should have been drifting from one of the three chimneys on the structure, since it was nearly the dinner hour. The corral was empty, too, its gate hanging open.

"It belonged to Sam, one of the Rangers buried in Bryant's Gap. He was close to retiring, aimed to settle in and work this spread. His wife had passed and all he had was his son. I assume Trace took it over."

The Indian's dark eyes narrowed. "It is too quiet. He was expecting you, but there is no one."

A sigh came from the Ranger's lips. A prickle of apprehension went through his nerves. Tonto was right, Trace Cooper knew they were due to arrive; the Ranger had asked Dan to send the rancher a telegram informing him they would reach the ranch by late afternoon on this day; someone should have been here to meet them. That the ranch appeared deserted was a bad sign.

"I don't like it, either, Tonto. Trace Cooper somehow made the connection to me and asked us here, and now there's no sign of life."

Tonto's gaze remained intent on the house. "If he knows who you are, he has information that would be of value to certain men, men like Butch Cavendish."

"But Cavendish is dead…"

"There were members of his gang that were never rounded up, Kemosabe."

The Lone Ranger's eyes hardened behind the half-mask. "They were followers, unlikely to think for themselves. They scattered when Cavendish died, likely joined other gangs. This…smacks of something else. If Cooper has gone missing, there's a good reason—and it has to do with whatever he summoned us here for. But that may have nothing to do with me."

The Indian shook his head. "You do not believe that, Kemosabe. I hear it in your voice."

The Ranger offered a weak smile. "My mind tells me I'm connecting threads of different colors…"

"But your instinct tells you they match."

25

The Ranger nodded. "I keep going over it in my mind, asking myself why Trace Cooper, if he does indeed know who I am, waited so long to contact me."

"Perhaps his life was peaceful until now and he had no need of you."

The Lone Ranger glanced at his friend. "Now I hear it in your voice. You don't believe that."

The Indian let a small smile touch his lips, as quickly gone. "No, I do not, Kemosabe."

"It doesn't make sense. Surely there were things about that day his father was killed he would have wanted to ask if he knew my identity all along, but he didn't. Which might mean he recently came across the information…and if he did…"

"Then perhaps someone else did as well…" Tonto shifted in his saddle but his gaze did not leave the hacienda. "The Potawatomi have a saying: Once the wolf scents blood he follows it forever. There is the scent of blood on the wind, Kemosabe. The wolf seeks you."

A small chill slid down the Ranger's spine. "I wish I could say you were wrong, but what I'm feeling…it's more than just being near Bryant's Gap again."

"Kemosabe…" Tonto's voice lowered and his eyes narrowed further. "I was unsure at first, but I saw movement within the house. We are being watched. The window to the right of the door…"

The Lone Ranger's gaze snapped in that direction. The late afternoon sun was dropping towards the horizon and shadows were lengthening from the house and outbuildings. Windows appeared like shiny ebony; he could see nothing beyond them. But he knew the man beside him had uncanny senses, honed by years on his own and with the Ranger. Those senses had saved his and the Ranger's lives too many times to warrant doubt.

"Ride, Kemosabe!" Tonto shouted suddenly, and the Lone Ranger saw it then—a glint of dying sunlight off metal.

He acted without hesitation, heels gigging the great white horse into motion. "Away, Silver!" He tugged the reins, sending the mount left. Beside him, Tonto had already heeled Scout in the opposite direction.

The move came in nearly the same instant a blast crashed from within the house. The shooter didn't bother lifting the window; glass exploded, shards spiraling, lacerating the air and raining to the grass as lead plowed through.

A bullet burrowed into the ground where the Lone Ranger had been an instant before.

He hunched low in the saddle and swung the horse in a zigzagging arc, making himself as difficult a target as possible. A second shot came, bullet whining through the air entirely too close to his head for comfort.

Someone *was* in the house, and that someone had been watching them, weighing their presence and concluding they had come for trouble. The mask. That had likely decided it. One of the hazards of preserving his anonymity and he couldn't blame folks for shooting first and questioning later, especially if something dire had happened at the ranch. The mask too often branded him a criminal.

Whoever was shooting was no outlaw, that much was obvious. An outlaw wouldn't have pondered the

27

situation; he would have shot immediately. The Ranger carried a reputation with owlhoots, one that put a bounty on his head for any outlaw with balls enough to claim it.

The Lone Ranger angled right, getting Silver behind the bunkhouse. He was out of the saddle in a heartbeat, an ivory-handled .45 appearing in his hand as if by magic. He eased around the corner of the building, bringing the gun up to the right side of his face, gloved finger feather-light on the trigger. Gaze sweeping the area, he decided getting near the house was going to be a problem. The shooter had a clear shot, if the Ranger came out into the open. The icehouse was a hundred feet distant, but he would be exposed for more time than he felt comfortable with, and in returning fire he had to take care; because if it wasn't an outlaw who'd fired on them, that meant it was possibly one of Cooper's ranchhands, someone innocent.

But he needed to chance it. He had no choice. Something had happened to Cooper and he owed it to the son of the Ranger who had died that day at Bryant's Gap to find out what. He needed to get close to the house, gain access and capture whoever was shooting at them.

He sought any sign of Tonto, but the Indian had seemingly disappeared. He spotted no sign of Scout, either.

Without further thought, he darted for the icehouse. He triggered shots as he ran, silver bullets chipping off pieces of adobe as they ricocheted from the wall around the window. He darted left, then right.

A blast came from the house; a bullet dug up dirt

28

inches from his fleeing bootheel. The icehouse was still fifty feet away.

He wasn't going to make it…

5

Seven days ago…
#

Things were going according to plan and once her man returned from town the Blood Creek Gang would make their next move.

She sat on a rock at the edge of camp, fireants crawling through her nerves again. She'd never been particularly patient; in fact, it damn near drove her loco waiting on things to work. She preferred action, taking what she wanted in a flurry of blood and gunsmoke. But vengeance on a man like Reid, this Lone Ranger, wasn't something that could be rushed. The man was a survivor; he'd proved that. Too well.

Yes, patience was what was needed to lure a man like that, to bring him here by striking at the few who might attract his attention. Patience. Butch had always told her she was lacking in such, and he was right.

But that didn't mean she couldn't kill somebody.

She pushed off her Stetson, to let it hang at her back. The night was moonless, but jittering light from the campfire bathed one side of her face. It was a hard face for a woman and she knew it. No one would have called her pretty, now, and no one would ever mistake her for one of them Eastern fancy women. Not that she gave a damn. Too many years selling her ass in saloons had etched deep lines about her ice-green eyes and thin-lipped mouth. The elements had scrubbed her skin raw and ruddy and the close-shorn haircut she had given herself with a Bowie knife did nothing to enhance her femininity. But it didn't matter a lick anymore. Nothing did, except revenge on the man who'd taken everything that meant anything to her.

That sonofabitch would pay. He'd learn what true loneliness was like—and then he'd die.

She spat a stream of saliva and tobacco juice, then dug the chaw out from between her lip and gum and flung it to the ground. The taste suddenly annoyed her; every gawdamned thing annoyed her. Especially that idjit, Trent. Where the hell was he, anyhow?

Behind her eight men sat about the fire. Some played poker while others drank bitter-brewed Arbuckle's. One slept, hat over his face. They were as motley a crew of bastards as Butch had ever assembled and while she rightly suspected they didn't cotton much to following a woman, they put up with it because they split the take from stage and bank robberies generously. And she'd blow anyone's brains out who defied her. She'd lost three men that way already, though it had been a fine and deadly lesson to the rest.

The sound of slowing hoofbeats pulled her from her thoughts and her head lifted and came around. She stood, hand brushing aside a flap of her duster, then resting on the handle of her Smith & Wesson.

The men behind her came to their feet, their hands also going to their guns.

"It's me," a man said as the hoofbeats drew to a halt and a rider emerged from the shadows of the night.

"Jesus H., Trent," she said, hand relaxing, though she had half a notion to shoot him just for the hell of it. "Took your own gawdamn time, didn't you? You been gone half the day."

The man named Trent, a young outlaw with orange-red hair cut short and a smear of freckles across a nose that showed evidence of having been broken somewhere in the past, dismounted, leading his horse to a cottonwood and tethering it to a branch. She had caught a look on his face she didn't much care for, a measure of defiance and disrespect he'd damn well best lose if he expected to go on living. The look had vanished by the time he turned back to her.

"Took longer to find out than I figgered," he said, removing his hat. "A-cause I saw Cooper ride into town." His voice irritated her. It had a scratchy quality that rode her nerves and she wondered why she had hired him in the first place. Was s'posed to be fast with a gun, but he was still on trial and a hair's breadth from being convicted and sentenced.

"What'd he do there?"

"He stopped by the marshal's to report a brand altering, then rode out to Bryant's Gap."

"Sonofabitch…" she muttered. "He saw the dug up graves?"

Trent nodded. "He saw them. Filled in five of them, too. Had himself a look on his face after."

"He knows…" Her voice came low, thoughtful.

"Knows what?" Trent asked. "I don't see what this has to do with anything anyway. We're wastin' time followin' folks around. We could be hittin' stages."

Her hand went to the handle of her gun again and

the hard lines on her face grew harder.

"I don't reckon you're questioning my judgment, are you?"

The expression on Trent's face said that was exactly what he was doing. She hoped he voiced it, because that would give her the excuse she needed. Trent apparently though better of it.

"No…no, I ain't. Just don't see what this is all about."

"It's about revenge, you stupid sonofabitch. That's all you need to know."

Trent stood stock still and his Adam's apple bobbed. He wanted to challenge her authority but was afeared of her and he'd damn well better be.

"What about the marshal?" she asked when he didn't say anything.

"I overheard him and his deputy," he said, words coming out a bit too fast and betraying his unease. "He's thinkin' about calling in the county marshal and his men. He reckons the store owner's killin' was the work of some gang. Someone saw you outside the store."

She rubbed a hand over her lower face, not at all pleased with the prospect. County men coming in here now would ruin everything. She'd misjudged things, hadn't thought anyone would pay her any mind outside the store.

"Well, we can't have that, now, can we?" she said.

"We ought to just ride—"

"The hell we will!" she said, her voice a whip. "Not until I finish what I came to do. Marshal Moore knew the Reids…" Her voice trailed off, thoughts shifting

33

through alternatives to her plan. She had reckoned on hitting the marshal after Cooper, but that had to be stepped up.

"The Reids?" Trent asked.

She gazed at him, flame in her eyes, then at the other men. "We're going to take the town, boys. We're takin' it tonight."

"The whole town?" one of her men asked, voice heavy with surprise.

"The whole gawdamned town. Congratulations, Parker…" She eyed the man who had spoken. "Time we're done hurrahing Coopersville; you're going to be the new marshal." She looked back to Trent. "Moore still in his office?"

The young outlaw nodded. "Deputy, too."

"Mount up. Trent, take Hawkins and secure the saloon. Fill anyone with lead who don't take to the notion. Rest of us will take care of the marshal and his man."

Worried looks passed between some of her men, but fifteen minutes later ten riders tore into Coopersville, two splitting off and galloping toward the saloon. She led the charge, reins twisted around one hand, the other unleashing her Smith & Wesson and triggering shots.

The men with her did the same. Lead punched into building walls and splintered wood from supporting beams. Windows exploded with jangling crashes under the barrage, glass raining to the boardwalks. Holes appeared in troughs, which spouted streams of water. Dust from pounding hoofs wafted up in dingy clouds.

Few folks were out and about; those who were became instantly sorry they hadn't headed for the safety of their homes a few moments earlier.

One of the outlaws took aim on a cowboy half in his cups staggering down the boardwalk. He blasted a shot and the man flew sideways, a gaping hole in his chest, and toppled over a rail into a water trough recently topped off with rain. Water splashed to the rutted hardpack.

The handful of remaining townsfolk on the boardwalks went down seconds behind him, only one getting out any kind of a yell before a bullet obliterated half his face.

The woman smiled an ice-cold smile and angled her mount toward the marshal's office. She counted off the seconds, knowing it would not be long.

She made it to three before the office door flew open. Marshal Moore, shock twisting his worn features, stepped out onto the boardwalk, Peacemaker drawn. He raised it, tried to fire on her but she was ready for it.

"Hi-yo, Silver, you sonofabitch…" she said and punctuated it with a vicious laugh, squeezed the trigger.

The marshal stuttered in his step, a blue hole suddenly appearing in his forehead. He went backwards, slammed into the deputy just coming out of the office behind him.

She fired again; the deputy, who'd caught the marshal in one arm, dropped the lawman. He coughed a crimson spray, stood stock still, as if uncertain what had happened. He tried to say something while pawing at his gun, but blood geysered from a hole in his throat.

Gagging, he pitched forward, crashed face-first to the boardwalk and lay still.

Just like that, it was over, and a measure of disappointment washed through her at how easy it had been. Lambs slaughtered by wolves.

She reined up, her men silencing their blasts and drawing up around her. Screams from the saloon, shrill and terror-stricken, cascaded into the night, followed by shots.

The town was hers. And soon, so would be the Lone Ranger.

6

"Git'em up, Scout!" Tonto yelled and heeled the pinto into a sprint toward the left side of the house. He had been studying the window to the right of the door, certain he'd glimpsed movement behind the dark glass. That notion was confirmed the moment sunlight glinted off the barrel of a rifle. It had to be a rifle, with the accuracy and range the shooter exhibited. They had been lucky, this time, not being hit, but whoever lurked within the homestead was still firing and that luck might just run out at any second.

He leaned forward in the saddle as he drove the mount in a looping arc toward the far end of the house, keeping low. But the shooter was not aiming at him; he was aiming at the man in the mask riding in the opposite direction. A glance over his shoulder told him the Ranger had made it to the shelter of the bunkhouse unscathed, but his friend would not be content to remain there, nor would he kill the man inside shooting at them. Sometimes Kemosabe took unnecessary chances, but he lived by a code, one Tonto respected, for it was much like the codes of his red brothers. A pity many others, both red and white, did not hold to their standards so strongly more often.

The Ranger would try to get into the house and capture the shooter; Tonto knew his ways well enough by now so that many plans between them went unspoken, only acted upon. But Kemosabe's reluctance to take life would make him vulnerable to a man with a rifle and an eagle eye.

Unless Tonto could do something to even the odds.

As he reached the far corner of the structure, he tugged on the reins. Scout slowed, angled sharply right, and Tonto was out of the saddle before the pinto came to a halt.

His moccasined feet hit the ground running. He bent, his steps seeming barely to touch the grass as he scooted toward the back of the hacienda. He did not want to be heard approaching and when he did not want to be heard no white man's ears could detect his presence.

Scout snorted, but stayed put at the side of the house. For as often as words went unspoken between Tonto and the Ranger, they did as well between Indian and his horse.

Tonto's gaze narrowed as he came around the back of the homestead. He had judged the shooter to be in a parlor or study at the front, which likely meant the kitchen was in the rear.

He doubled lower, keeping below the level of the windows, chancing a glance in each as he passed beneath them. Twenty feet on, he stopped, straightened and pressed himself to the wall next to the third window. The kitchen. He knew it without looking inside. Someone had thrown scraps of food out the window; likely a cook seeking to feed birds and small animals. Crumbs and a few chicken bones littered the ground.

Easing around, he chanced a look into the room,

confirming that it was indeed the kitchen. The room appeared utterly deserted. He pressed his hand to the glass, applying just enough pressure to move the window upward a fraction. Whoever had tossed out the scraps of food had left it unlocked.

Shots came from the front and his heart leaped. He was running out of time. Under cover of another blast he thrust the window upward, holding his breath on the expectation of any loud squeak the window might make, despite himself. But it went up soundlessly and he let out the breath, thankful to Kichimanido for small blessings.

His entrance was as silent as the window's rising. He padded across the floor, skirting a counter island above which hung copper pots and pans. He noted unprepared food on the counter, as if whoever were about to start the evening meal had suddenly walked off and left it. A slab of beefsteak was gray and buzzing with flies. The stench of decay soured the air.

Those at the ranch had been interrupted abruptly and that was not a good sign. Was the shooter in the front room responsible for that departure?

Tonto doubted that to be the case. If so, why remain behind? No, whoever was firing belonged here and was doing so out of self-preservation and fear.

At the kitchen entryway, Tonto paused, listened. Sounds of movement came from the front of the house during a lull in the shooting.

He glided into a lone hallway beside which a center stairway rose to a wrought-iron railed mezzanine hall above. He noticed a brown stain on the floor halfway down. Blood. Someone had been wounded or

39

perished in this hallway.

A noise came from a room at his left a few yards ahead. He slipped along the white-washed wall upon which hung a painting of an older woman and man wearing a Texas Ranger's uniform. A gold plate on the bottom of the frame said, Adelaide and Samuel Cooper.

Reaching the entry ahead, Tonto paused against the wall, eased his head around the corner to peer into a large parlor.

The parlor was in a shambles. Chairs and settee were overturned. Another painting, this of Samuel Cooper, hung askew above the fireplace. Chips had been gouged by bullets from the mantle and adobe walls. Lamps lay shattered on the floor.

Tonto froze, a wave of ice water washing through him. Blood. So much blood, splattered and dried, on the polished floorboards and staining an expensive carpet that appeared to be of some middle-eastern origin. Someone had perished in this room, and his heart ached for Kemosabe. His friend had lost enough of those he cared about. Now there would be another loss; Tonto felt certain of it.

Gunshots echoed from beyond the house; bullets hit the frame around the window outside with muffled hammering sounds. The Ranger was making some sort of move. Movement came from the window and Tonto's dark eyes locked on a man poised there clutching a Winchester. The man appeared haggard, hair disheveled and chin stubbled with three days beard growth. His movements appeared jerky, frantic. This man was not an outlaw; he was frightened. He was dressed in heavy work clothes, denims and canvas shirt. A ranchhand, Tonto would have guessed.

The man jammed the muzzle of the rifle through the broken pane in preparation to fire. He levered a shell into the chamber, blasted a shot.

Tonto flung himself into the room, using the blast to cover any sounds he made doing so.

The shooter fired again, then suddenly came up and around, as if some animal instinct had alerted him to the Indian's presence. A reflection, Tonto knew, in the remaining panes, had warned the man.

The shooter swung the Winchester toward Tonto. The Indian leaped before the man could aim properly, came down next to the shooter. The rifle blasted, the sound deafening in the confined area. The bullet shrieked to Tonto's left, ricocheted from the adobe wall across the room, taking a chunk of plaster with it.

With both hands, Tonto grabbed the rifle barrel, yanking as he threw himself backward and down. His back rounded as it hit the floor and his legs snapped up, jamming into the shooter's belly as the man came down atop him.

The shooter, propelled by an explosive thrust from Tonto's legs, hurtled over the Indian and crashed to the floor on his back. Tonto had retained his hold on the Winchester. He sprang to his feet, hurled the rifle aside.

The shooter struggled to come to his feet, eyes glazed and terror-stricken as they locked on the Indian.

"Kill me, Injun!" he shouted, as he reached his feet. "That's what you came here to do! That's what you all came here to do, to kill us all!"

"I am not here to kill," Tonto said.

41

"The hell you ain't!" The man lunged, fist swinging.

Tonto sidestepped, countered with a right that clacked the man's teeth together and snapped his head back.

The shooter fell against the overturned settee, all fight drained out of him. He gazed up, eyes watery with tears.

"What happened here?" Tonto asked, voice soothing, but the man began to weep as sounds came from the front door.

7

Three days ago…
#

The room above the saloon she had made their headquarters was smaller than she would have liked but it would have to do for now. But if there was one thing she despised more than waiting it was being caged, and being stuck in a room above the saloon with nine men was akin to the Devil's own Hell, not that some of them didn't find other arrangements with the whores at night.

They had taken the town and put the fear of sudden violent death in the townsfolk. Fewer than she would have liked had been killed and that was going to have to be remedied. Something about the sight and bitter-copper scent of spilled blood aroused her, enflamed every part of her being. But for the time being she would need some other outlet.

Her gaze shifted to the other men in the room, five of them, four others having been sent out to keep an eye on things and make sure no brave soul took the gawdamned stupid notion to try to call in the county law. There was only one man attached to justice she wanted riding in here—and that man wore a mask.

The men sat around a small table near the window, playing poker, dirty sunlight spilling across the cards.

The room was grimy, sparsely furnished with a bed with a brass frame and worn mattress, a night table atop which sat a kerosene lamp and a bureau holding a porcelain pitcher and wash basin.

"Get out," she said, rising from the hardbacked chair and shucking her hat. She tossed it onto a bedpost.

"What?" one of the men said, looking up from his cards.

"I said, get out, all of you. Don't come back for an hour. Entertain yourselves with some of the whores."

The men looked at each other, then tossed their cards to the table and stood. They knew better than to question her orders when she took to these moods.

"'Cept you," she said, looking to the youngest of the outlaws. He was the only one with a lick of good looks.

A glint of worry sparked in his eyes and one of the other men uttered a vicious knowing chuckle on his way out.

After they'd left, she unbuckled her gunbelt, tossed it onto a chair. The remaining outlaw shifted feet, eyes roving.

She gave him the smile of a snake about to swallow a mouse.

"Relax, Matthews. You'll enjoy it more."

"Enjoy what?" he asked, voice low.

She uttered a vapid laugh. "Enjoy putting your pecker to use…" She unbuttoned the top three buttons of her shirt, and the young outlaw stared, something akin to panic on his face.

"Hit me," she said.

"What?"

"Hit me, you stupid sonofabitch. I like it rough. Butch always gave it to me rough."

Matthews hesitated, then his hand came up, striking her full across the face.

She laughed, the sound riddled with mockery. "That the best you got, peckerwood?" With her nails, she raked his face and the outlaw let out a startled sound. "Harder!"

He obliged, anger in his eyes and trickles of blood leaking from the scratches on his cheek. His fist crashed into her jaw. She went backwards and down, ended up sitting against the bed, one arm draped up on the edge of the mattress. Blood snaked from the corner of her mouth. She swiped at it with the back of her hand and her dazed ice-green eyes looked up at the young outlaw.

"Now that's more like it, cowboy…"

She damn near killed the young outlaw in the next half hour, she reckoned. The young ones never quite expected what was coming, how insatiable in her cravings she could be. The scratches on his face had been merely a prelude. By the time she finished he looked like he'd tangled with a gawdamn mountain cat.

She lay beside him on the bed, tangled in a worn sheet, figuring on going again, despite the fact the peckerwood looked damn near wore out, when the door burst open.

Trent stood on the threshold, shock sweeping across his ruddy face as his gaze locked on the two figures on the mattress.

"Jesus Christ, Trent," she said, swinging her legs

out of bed, turning her back to him. The young outlaw scrambled for his clothing and quickly dressed.

"Well?" she asked, finding her own clothes and beginning to dress. Trent seemed transfixed not on the sight of her body, but on the map of scars marring her back. Beatings, some terrible and some pleasurable, had put them there. She suspected Trent wasn't the kind for a woman anyhow, and the thought of that sickened her, which was saying something, a-cause not much could anymore.

As she strapped on her gunbelt, Trent finally found his voice. The younger outlaw she'd just finished with stood near the night stand, shifting feet and staring at the floor.

"Cooper…he came into town and went to the telegraph office. Sent a telegram."

Her ice-green eyes narrowed on him. "What did he send and who did he sent it to?"

"I don't know." Trent's voice came with a sudden hitch.

Her face hardened. Gawdamn, he was useless. "You don't know?" Her voice dropped and death swelled in her eyes. "Didn't it gawdamn occur to you to get a copy of the slip after he left?"

Trent's face reddened. "Don't see how it matters none. Don't see how any of it does."

Defiance. Plain and infuriating in his tone.

"I'm right sick of you questioning my motives all the time, not to mention your stupidity, you sorry sonofabitch."

Trent's face went from red to purple. Anger flashed in his eyes. "And I'm right sick of you wastin' our time

46

on nothin'. You're jest a woman, for chrissakes. You got no call leadin' this gang."

She stood stock still for a moment, openly surprised the spineless fool had come out with it. She almost laughed, except she could not have any of her men speaking to her that way. What kind of an example would it set?

Trent never had the chance to draw. Her Smith & Wesson was out of its holster and belching flame and gray smoke before he could blink. He flew backwards across the hall, crashed into the opposite wall and landed on his belly on the floor, a bullet in his heart.

She holstered the gun, glanced at the young outlaw, whose face was white with shock. These men were hard; she was harder.

"Get rid of him. Now."

She left the room, giving Trent's head a kick as she departed.

Five minutes later, she entered the telegraph office. A smallish man with a green visor came half out of his seat. Her gun was out and aimed, stopping him before he could say a word. Thunder filled the little room and he tumbled backward over his chair and landed hard on his back, unmoving.

She holstered her gun, then went to a pile of slips stabbed onto a spindle, searched through them until she located the one she wanted, the one sent by Trace Cooper.

A low laugh came from her lips. "Jesus, you really did figure it out, didn't you, Cooper?" The recipient's name stopped her short: Dan Reid. It was addressed to Dan Reid. But Dan Reid was dead. That was one body she had seen.

A relative, perhaps? A son?

"Sonofabitch…" she muttered. This was better than she could have hoped for. She hadn't known how long it might take to lure the Ranger here by striking at possible links, but happenstance had provided her with a direct line to him—and to the sole surviving Reid relative. She would have to pay him a visit once her work here was done.

It was turning out to be a good day, indeed.

8

A bullet whined past the Lone Ranger's ear as he dashed for the icehouse now a mere twenty-five feet away. He returned fire, pelting the window frame with silver, but it did little to deter the man inside.

Another shot followed, but the Ranger had already doubled, hurled himself forward. Lead shrieked through empty air where the Masked Man had been an instant before.

He tucked himself into a ball as he went down, landed on a shoulder and rolled. In nearly the same move he sprang up again, triggering another shot at the window.

Ten feet.

His breath beat out and his heart quickened. A few more steps and he'd reach the icehouse. Within the hacienda the rifle went silent. Behind the half-mask, the Ranger's eyes narrowed. He reached the corner of the icehouse, flattened himself against its wall.

Breathing rapid, he chanced a look around the corner, eyes probing the window from which the man had been shooting.

Nothing. No sign of movement. Was the shooter waiting for him to expose himself to fire again? It seemed unlikely, given the frantic shots to this point.

"You there!" he yelled. "In the house! I'm a

friend."

No sound or shot came back. His gaze sought to pierce the interior of the house, but the sun's angle was wrong, too low, and he could see nothing.

He waited, counting off ten seconds. He was going to have to chance a move toward the house. The fortresslike front door appeared slightly ajar and that puzzled him.

Easing around the corner, gun raised to his cheek, he readied to hurl himself backward at the slightest sign of movement and gunfire.

But none came. He stood there, gave it another ten seconds, leaving himself open. Still no shots came.

He started forward, every sense alert, prepared for a lunge left or right, but the caution proved unnecessary. He noticed the icehouse door was ajar also and paused, poked the barrel of his .45 into the inch gap between door and frame and eased it open. The door shrieked like a coffin lid rising and with what met his sight, they might as well have been one and the same.

"My God..." he said, voice heavy with horror and melancholy. He quickly closed the door, an ungodly odor assailing his nostrils, one he felt certain he would not be able to get out of his memory for a long time to come.

In motion again, he drifted toward the house, dread cinching his belly. They had ridden for the ranch as soon as possible, made good time, but it was still too late. With what he had seen in the icehouse he was certain of that fact.

When he reached the door, that suspicion was strengthened. It was ajar because a bullet had shattered the lock. He pressed a black-gloved palm flat against the door, sent it swinging inward.

Inside the house, the silence felt thick, oppressive, as if he had stepped into a boneyard instead of a place where men lived and worked. Then weeping reached his ears, coming from the parlor to his right.

The Lone Ranger went to the parlor, took in the scene with a glance and frowned. Tonto was helping a man to his feet. The Indian righted the settee, urged the weeping man onto it. He cast the Ranger a glance, then went to where the Winchester had landed and picked it up. He placed it on a small table.

The Ranger stepped into the room and the shooter suddenly spotted him. He leaped to his feet, terror sweeping over his face.

"Murderers!" the man screamed. "Killers! Come back to finish the job? This time you can kill me, too!"

"We are not here to kill anyone," the Ranger said. "We were asked to help."

The man appeared to have a hard time digesting the words. Fear gripped him and he saw and heard everything through its filter. "You, you're wearing a mask. You're an outlaw."

"I'm no outlaw. This mask represents justice. You're one of Cooper's men?"

The man nodded, relaxing a hair as the Ranger holstered his gun. "I'm the ranch foreman, Brent…least, I was…"

"Trace Cooper asked me here, Mr. Brent. We…go back a long ways. Where is he?"

"Gone." Brent collapsed onto the settee, burying his face in his hands. Sobs wracked his body.

51

"What do you mean, 'gone', Mr. Brent?" the Ranger asked, voice steady, calm, despite the dread gripping him. He'd learned too well to hide sorrow since that fateful day at Bryant's Gap. Sometimes he wondered if he could even still feel things the way normal men did.

"They took him," Brent said, hands dropping as his head lifted and he peered up at the Lone Ranger.

"Where are the rest of the ranchhands?" Tonto asked. "The cook?"

"Dead," the Lone Ranger said, face grim. "The bodies are in the icehouse. I saw them before I came in. Some were shot up so bad they were unrecognizable."

"I put them in there," Bent said, voice quivering. "I didn't know what else to do. Can't go to the marshal for help."

The Lone Ranger's brow furrowed beneath the half-mask. "Marshal Moore? He's a good man."

"Was," Brent said. "He's dead, too. The gang killed him. Killed the general store owner, Sanders, as well, least Trace figured they did. New marshal's one of the gang. They got the whole town in terror."

The Lone Ranger cast Tonto an uneasy glance. "Trace Cooper, Moore, Sanders…" His voice came low, almost a whisper. All those men had known the Reids. The notion sent a chill down his spine.

"They took Trace Cooper?" the Ranger asked. "Where?"

The foreman shrugged, and with the back of his hand swiped tears from his face. "I don't know. They came in here like hellfire. We never had a chance. They just started killing and killing."

"How did you survive, Mr. Brent?" Tonto asked.

The foreman's head dropped and for suspended moments he remained silent, shuddering. When at last he looked up, pain laced his blood-shot eyes.

"I'm a coward, Mister," he said, guilt and regret fighting in his voice. "I hid upstairs when the shooting started. I don't know why, but I did. I saw men die, men I worked with and lived with everyday. I saw them carry out Cooper unconscious and leave that—" The foreman ducked his chin toward a table flush against the wall.

The Lone Ranger went to it, picked up the single object that lay atop it. After examining it a moment, he tossed it to Tonto, who caught it.

"Copper bullet..." Tonto said, brow furrowing.

"This gang have a name?" the Lone Ranger asked, turning back to the foreman.

The man nodded. "Called themselves the Blood Creek Gang."

The dread the Lone Ranger had felt earlier increased tenfold. "What did you say?" His voice came barely audible and he swallowed against a knot of emotion in his throat. It was a name he had never expected to hear again.

"Copper Widow," the man repeated. "The leader made a point of saying it."

"But the Blood Creek Gang no longer exists," Tonto said, fire behind his dark eyes.

"Tell that to the dead men in the icehouse," Brent said. "Tell that to their kin."

"You get a good look at the leader?" the Ranger asked.

53

The foreman shook his head. "Saw him from the back. Had a hat pulled low and wore a duster. Small fella, sounded real young. Had a voice like a young boy. Didn't know better I might even have thunk it was a girl."

The Ranger moved to the entryway and Tonto followed suit, tucking the copper bullet into a pocket of his buckskins.

"We need to find Cooper," the Lone Ranger said. "He's a lead back to Dan and if they make him talk…"

Tonto nodded. "How, Kemosabe? The Gang has the town. He could be anywhere or dead."

"I don't know at this point. But I will." He swung his attention back to the foreman. "You have family you can go to, Mr. Brent? You're just making yourself a target staying here."

The foreman shook his head. "No, no one. I got no one. Cooper and the boys was my family. I let them down."

"There was a whole gang, Mr. Brent," the Ranger said, his tone sympathetic. The man felt guilty enough; no use questioning his courage, now. "You had tried to stop them you'd be in the icehouse with the rest."

"Why?" Brent asked, eyes pleading.

"Why, what, Mr. Brent?" the Ranger said.

"Why am I alive when the rest are all dead? Why am I the lone survivor? I don't deserve it. I don't deserve—"

They couldn't have stopped him. Brent was suddenly off the settee and grabbing the Winchester from the table.

"No!" the Ranger yelled, both he and Tonto step-

54

ping toward the foreman.

Brent levered a shell into the chamber, swung the Winchester around and jammed the barrel deep into his mouth. His finger jerked the trigger.

The blast shuddered through the room and half his face became a pulpy mass of spraying flesh, bone and blood. He collapsed, the Winchester hitting the floor next to him.

"My God..." the Lone Ranger muttered, nausea tightening his belly.

Tonto's hand went to the Lone Ranger's shoulder. "He could not live with his guilt, Kemosabe. It would have been slow torturous death for a man such as he."

The Ranger nodded, wondering in that moment what made him so different from the dead man on the floor and finding the answer suddenly elusive.

9

Two days ago…
#

The ranchhouse appeared peaceful in the breaking dawn. The sun painted the grass with gold and glinted like sparkling diamonds from water troughs and window panes. A breeze carried the scents of bacon and coffee. White smoke wafted from the hacienda's chimneys and a few 'hands moved about the grounds, preparing for the day's chores.

So serene. So mundane. It disgusted her, and soon the morning gold would run with scarlet.

She sat her horse on the outskirts of the Cooper ranch, eight other men reined up around her. Grim anticipation glinted in their eyes. Bloodlust.

"Branch off," she told her men. "On my signal. I want no one left breathin' to tell the tale—except Trace Cooper. We take him alive."

"Why?" asked one of the men, the one known as Parker.

She glanced back at the outlaw, hands tightening with annoyance on the reins. "Trent asked a lot of stupid questions, too…"

The outlaw's face washed pale, the threat in her tone plain. "Reckon I don't need to know," he mumbled.

"Reckon you don't," she said. Fact was, she wanted Trace Cooper for two things: Cooper had figured out the Ranger's identity; he knew Dan Reid and where he was located. She wanted that information. He was also bait for the Masked Man and that savage he rode with.

"You're coming with me," she said, glancing at Matthews, the gouges still livid on his face. It appeared a struggle for him not to cringe at the order, and she decided once she got tired of him, which, as was her habit, would be soon, she would end his employment with the gang violently.

"Yah!" she yelled, spurs gouging into her mount's sides. The big bay shot toward the ranchhouse. Behind her, outlaws gigged their horses into motion, half going right, the other half sweeping left. The young outlaw followed her lead.

The blood fever burned in her veins and her heart quickened in anticipation of the kill. Shots rang out, shattering the serene morning. The few ranchhands out on the grounds were caught unawares. They fell under a hail of lead.

The bunkhouse door flew open and men poured out, some half-dressed, wearing long underwear. Roused by the commotion they tumbled out unarmed and she laughed, an insane cackling thing, as her men fired on them, wholesale slaughter. The air filled with the scent of blood and gunsmoke and it enraptured her. She felt alive again, as alive as she had with Butch. She let out a whoop, yanking hard on the reins as she neared the hacienda.

She jumped from the saddle before the horse came to a complete stop. The younger outlaw reined up behind her, dismounted. Both drew guns.

The gunfire that crashed through the early morning seemed never-ending. It rang out like the roaring cackles of demons. Men, wounded, shrieked, went abruptly silent as their bullet-riddled bodies crumpled to the dew-wet grass. Plumes of gray smoke drifted across the compound.

She took the steps to the veranda in a single bound, her man following. Up came her Smith & Wesson, finger tightening on the trigger, blasting a shot. Lead mangled the door lock. She kicked the door inward, entered a small foyer.

A woman in a cook's uniform was halfway down the hall to the left of the center staircase.

The Smith & Wesson shuddered with another blast and the cook bounded backwards, her ragged body sprawling on the hall floor, where it lay still.

She uttered a satisfied laugh. Behind her the young outlaw fired, obliterating the head of an older male servant stepping from the parlor. The old man was dead before his body hit the floor. The young outlaw stared at what he had done, eyes cold.

"What the hell, you feeling squeamish?" she asked, noting his pause.

He shook his head. "Cut the head off a chicken once. It danced around afterward for half an hour. Was hoping to see that with a man."

She laughed, a dead sound. Maybe she'd let him live after all. She liked his spunk.

He started towards the staircase, but she halted him with an upraised arm.

"Thought I saw something move up there," he said.

"Forget it. I see what I came for." She stepped toward the parlor, duster whipping about her legs. A man in his early thirties dressed in a silk morning robe, came from near the window, a Winchester in his hands. Shock had frozen his face into hard lines. He jerked up the rifle.

"Uh-uh," she said, leveling her gun on him. "'Less you're feelin' today's your day to meet your Maker."

"Who the hell are you?" he said through gritted teeth. "What are you doing in my home?"

"Drop the rifle," she said, gesturing with the gun.

The young man complied, setting the Winchester on a table.

Outside, the shooting had stopped. She could only assume that meant there were no survivors.

"I asked you who you were…" Trace Cooper's voice came steady, without fear.

She stepped up to him, smiled. "Why, we're the Blood Creek Gang, ain't you heard?" A laugh punctuated her statement and Trace Cooper didn't change expression.

"There's someone coming who'll deal with the likes of you," he said with such seriousness she wanted to laugh again.

She swung her gun with sudden violent force. It thudded against Trace Cooper's temple and he fell to the floor.

"Aware of that," she said. "And it's exactly what I want." Her hand went to a pocket in her coat, came out with a copper bullet. She tossed it to a small table flush against the wall. "Exactly what I want…"

10

The Lone Ranger's hands tightened on Silver's reins hard enough to make his forearms ache as he and Tonto rode into Bryant's gap. His body went rigid in the saddle and a memory painted in blood and amber shuddered through his mind. It was no dream what had happened here those many years ago. Five men had lost their lives, gunned down in cold blood by a madman named Butch Cavendish and his gang. But one had lived; one had buried his identity in an empty grave and behind a mask. One had vowed to bring justice to the Blood Creek Gang and spread a message across the West, one that promised those who robbed and killed they were not above the law and there was no place they could hide that the Lone Ranger would not find them.

His mission; his vow; his promise to his brother and to those Rangers who perished here that day.

He slowed the great white horse to an easy gait, Tonto doing the same beside him. The Indian glanced at him, concern on his face.

"You are troubled returning to this place, Kemosabe…"

"I am…I feel them, Tonto. Those ghosts you spoke of."

"There are no ghosts here, Kemosabe," Tonto said with a slight shake of his head. "You brought their killers to justice. Those men you rode with, your brother…they are at peace. You are haunted by your memories."

The Lone Ranger gazed at his friend, frowned. "Perhaps you're right. Whoever struck at Cooper and the others, they've unearthed those memories."

"Somebody has lured you to this place of death. Somebody uses the name of your enemy's gang and attacks those with a connection to your old identity."

The Ranger nodded. "But who? And why? I'm no closer to finding those answers. I just have more questions, and more death."

The Indian's gaze grew intense on the landscape ahead. "Perhaps more importantly, whom will they strike next?"

"I'm here now. Perhaps they'll strike at me." In truth, he was more worried they would strike at the man riding beside him. They were killing those from his past, men with only passing connections, old acquaintances. But this man beside him…he would die before he let them kill Tonto.

The Lone Ranger's gaze lifted to the gnarled rocky walls of the canyon, swept along the ridge to either side in search of any signs of bushwhackers. Bright copper sunlight glared down, sparkled from mica embedded in the rock but not from rifle or gun barrels that might pinpoint lurking ambushers. Whoever was behind all this had not chosen today for a confrontation. Though the gang leader was by now expecting the Ranger to take notice and come, he had no way of knowing he and Tonto would be here, at Bryant's Gap, to lay a trap.

I'm gonna be a Ranger someday, Dan—a Texas Ranger! You'll see!

Another memory rose up, this one in warm shades of yesterday, and a thin smile drifted across his lips.

Two boys of ten and thirteen, himself and his brother. He'd whittled a gun and a crude wooden star out of a piece of cottonwood branch.

"Maybe I'll be a Ranger, too," Dan said, his brother's young voice echoing from the past. They'd gone down to the riverbank after finishing chores on a bright Saturday morning. "You know you don't do nuthin' 'less I do it first!"

"That ain't so!" his young self said.

"Is so!" Dan said.

"You be the outlaw!" he said. "And I'll chase you down!"

"Why do I gotta be the outlaw?" Dan asked, scrunching up his freckled face.

"'Cause I have the gun." He held up the wooden toy, as if that emphatically ended the argument.

"Hell and tarnation," Dan said. "That ain't no reason!"

The younger boy gave his brother a look of reproach. "Pa'll switch your britches somethin' awful if'n he hears you cussin' like that."

Dan laughed. "You won't tell him."

"Why not?"

"'Cause I'll switch yours if you do."

"Say, that's outlaw talk, hombre. You best be ready to git out of town 'fore sundown if'n you know what's good fer ya."

"Kemosabe?" Tonto's voice penetrated the Lone Ranger's thoughts and again the rock-strewn canyon floor lay before his vision.

"Just…recollecting, Tonto," he said, melancholy lacing his tone and lingering in his soul. "Dan ended up becoming a Ranger before I did. I'd almost decided to start a cattle ranch. I'd grown out of my boyhood dreams, but Dan never forgot. I think he saw more in me than I saw in myself. I wonder, if I could go back, if I changed my decision to follow him…would he still be alive?"

"You cannot change what has been, Kemosabe. You can only shape what is to be. If it were not so the ghosts of my people would not ride the night skies."

"I suppose you're right." The Lone Ranger sighed, heart heavy. "But I wish I could change that day. I never trusted that man, Collins. If I had done more…"

"What could you have done?"

The Lone Ranger shrugged. "I wish I knew."

They rode onward another hundred yards, and the Lone Ranger's unease increased the closer they came to the spot he and the other Rangers had met with doom. Tonto was right: he could not go back and change what had happened, and nothing he could have done that day would have prevented what occurred.

He reined up, Tonto following suit, and stared at the six graves ahead. Beside the graves, a boulder- and scrub brush-littered trail wound up to the left ridge, and again he surveyed both sides of the canyon top and the trail itself, spotting nothing out of the ordinary, nothing to indicate any sign of another ambush.

He dismounted, muscles stiff from tension. He laid a gloved hand on Silver's neck. "Stay, big fella," he whispered, then walked to the graves.

Tonto stepped from the saddle, followed him. When the Lone Ranger reached the graves, he knelt. Five of them had been recently filled in, but the sixth was still open. He scooped up a handful of earth and let it trickle through his gloved fingers.

"The graves were dug up," he said, swiveling his head and gazing up at Tonto. "Then these five were re-filled." He stood, brushed dust off his glove.

"Cooper?" Tonto's dark eyes swept over the five mounds and one empty grave.

"I'm betting Cooper filled them in. He probably came out to visit his father's grave and found them open. He saw five bodies...Trace Cooper was always a smart hombre. He figured out the connection between me and the empty grave. That's why he sent the telegram."

"Someone else figured it out, too," Tonto said.

The Lone Ranger frowned, giving the Indian a slight nod. "I would have expected somebody like Cavendish to put it together. I think he half did before I showed him my face right before he died. That's why he asked me to take off the mask."

"But like you say, Butch Cavendish is dead. He took the knowledge of your identity to his grave."

"Yes...he did. But if he ever mentioned his suspicions to anyone..."

The Lone Ranger straightened, walked to the empty grave, peered down into it, as if he were gazing into a black screen of his past. In his mind he heard the gunfire and shouts of that day, heard the agonized sounds of the dying, and saw his brother perish before his eyes.

"Why?" he said over his shoulder to Tonto.

"Why?" the Indian said, face sympathetic but puzzled.

"That's what the foreman, Brent, asked us before he killed himself. Why me, Tonto? Why did I live and these five other men die? What makes me any better than them? What gave me the right to survive?"

The Indian looked at the ground, silent for dragging moments. Then his gaze rose. "You were chosen, Kemosabe. By the Kichimanido or by the white man's God or by pure Fate. You were chosen because of what your brother saw inside you that you did not see. You among men have the spirit to right the wrongs you see, the wrongs of other men. You were chosen to help those who would be prey to men such as Cavendish. You were chosen because your spirit refused to die and let others suffer. You were chosen because of those men that day, of all men, you alone would be able to accept and stand by the task to be put before you. You, Kemosabe…you Lone Ranger…"

The Lone Ranger's head lifted and he suppressed the emotion choking his throat. The events of that day were like a puzzle and once the pieces were fitted together the picture was of a man driven to bring outlaws to justice, to protect the innocent and give his life for his duty to help others. His brother had seen it; Tonto had seen it. Indeed, after all these years, he saw it in himself.

"I want the leader of this gang, Tonto. There's been enough death."

"Do we fill in grave?" Tonto nudged his chin towards the open hole.

The Lone Ranger shook his head. "Not yet. Someone knows who I am. That someone, when I bring them in, won't be inclined to keep it a secret any longer."

"Perhaps…"

"No, Tonto. If we can take him alive, we will. Stopping a murderer is more important than my secret. If exposure's the price I have to pay…then to hell with hiding…"

11

The present…

#

He was here. The Ranger. She knew it. She could feel it in her bones. The minutes were ticking away until her revenge. It wouldn't be long before that masked man came in here looking for her, though she knew he rightly had no idea who she was or even that she was a woman.

He would go to the Cooper ranch first, having been summoned there, and find the bodies, determine that Cooper was missing. He would put it together that Cooper, alive and in the hands of the enemy, posed a risk to this Dan Reid the rancher had telegraphed. Perhaps that danger would make the Ranger act in haste, make a mistake. But she couldn't count of that. He hadn't survived this long by being stupid.

The morning sun was already high overhead and the day was getting gawdamn hot. Heat waves rippled off the hardpacked wide main street. Cooperville was a sprawling town built akin to a horseshoe with false fronted buildings and homesteads at the south end of clapboard, brick and adobe. A gunshop, mercantile, bank, café and sundry businesses lined either side of the street.

She had just exited the café after a breakfast of

beefsteak, eggs and Arbuckle's. Awake most of the night ridin' Matthews had left her famished and him sawing wood loud enough to wake the dead. She'd made her other men find their own sleeping arrangements for the night.

She stepped off the boardwalk, eyed the bank, which was open for business. For now she'd let it be, despite objections from a couple of her men. But once her business with the Ranger was concluded she'd be payin' it a visit.

What once would have been a bustling cow town was more akin to a ghost town. Folks were plumb scared and she liked it that way. Made them less prone to stupidity, such as tryin' to bring in the county law. She killed one of them a day at random to make certain they got the message. She reckoned the wife of the bank man would be next, that prissy little bitch. She hadn't liked the woman on first look, and that never boded well for a long life.

She sauntered across the street, in no particular hurry, to the opposite boardwalk. The air smelled of horse piss and dust and the heat made it worse. Her nerves started to crawl. She was tired of stayin' in that room but she reckoned this would be the last time she could move freely about with the Ranger nearby. She wasn't ready to engage him just yet, no, not until she had that Injun and what she wanted from Cooper.

Cooper was a tough sonofabitch, she had to give him that. He hadn't talked, and by Christ she had tried to make him. She'd already pulled off a couple of his finger nails and beat him half to death. She might respect that in another life.

Stepping onto the opposite boardwalk, a passerby, a man, gave her wide berth, keeping his gaze pinned to the boards as he passed. A low laugh came from her lips.

"Don't worry, ain't your day," she yelled after him, but he didn't look back, only hurried his pace.

It was funny…she couldn't recollect what fear felt like. She'd known loneliness since she lost Butch, known it intimately. She knew hate and anger and disgust. She knew wrath and the craving for vengeance. But not fear. She had not known fear since the day her pa had lost her virginity to one of his drunken friends in a poker game. That was the first time she had felt fear…and the last. She had sworn the moment she ran away from that no-good bastard no one would take anything from her or make her afraid again. Never. In her years before Butch, as a bar whore, she had been the one to take—money from men who were too drunk to know their peckers were locked between her thighs and not where they intended them to be, and lives from those who got on her bad side, which were many and often. No man controlled her nor owned her. She controlled them and she reckoned that might be the one good thing she could thank her pa for. Fact, she had thanked him…right before put a bullet in him one night when he passed out upstairs in a whore's cubicle. He'd not even had the decency to recognize the woman he was trying to bed was his own daughter.

Then she'd met Butch. And everything had changed. She still took what she wanted—gold, jewels, sex, but she took it together with him. He was the cruelest sonofabitch she'd ever met up with, and she the meanest thing a man like Butch Cavendish ever had the good sense to keep around.

Gawdammit, she missed that peckerwood.

She shook off the memory as she reached the marshal's office. As she flung open the door, two of her men, one wearing a marshal's tin star and the other a deputy's badge, nearly came off their chairs. They would have had it not been for the whores sitting on their laps.

"You," she said to the blonde bar dove straddling Parker, the fake marshal. "Get out."

The girl quickly extricated herself from the man and, brushing blonde ringlets from her face, ran out the door.

"What about me?" the brunette woman wearing a peek-a-boo blouse asked, slipping off the deputy. She had a horse face that was entirely ugly.

"You...I don't like. Sorry." She pulled her Smith & Wesson and shot the woman in the head. The woman folded without uttering a sound, thudded hard on the floor.

"Jesus, what'd you go and do that for?" the fake deputy said, staring at the body of the dove. "I liked that one."

She holstered her gun. "Such is life. Both of you stop the whores and be on the alert. He's here."

"Who's here?" asked the marshal.

She smiled a vicious smile. "Reckon it's time I told you what we're doin' here and who we're doin' it to. I aim to kill the Lone Ranger..."

12

The afternoon sun was just starting to dip towards the western hills when the Lone Ranger and Tonto rode into Coopersville. Since he still had little idea what exactly he was facing, the Masked Man had decided to ride directly into town, throw down the gauntlet and try to force a move on the part of the gang. The notion was not as reckless as it first appeared. Whoever led the gang had struck all around the Ranger, at folks he had come in contact with and cared about in his former life. That meant for the moment the gang leader only desired to lure him close before putting into motion the final part of his plan. Otherwise the gang would have tried to ambush him on the trail.

No, this smacked of more than just the simple killing of a man who delivered justice to owlhoots. It smacked of something personal, a vendetta. Which meant the person tasking him would need him to know why he was being killed before actually doing the deed.

But that didn't apply to the man riding beside him. The Ranger saw only two choices to continue the pattern: killing Dan Reid and Tonto. Dan was safe as long as Cooper didn't talk, but the Ranger had no way of knowing whether the gang had forced the information from the rancher by now. Even if they had, he judged Dan would be secure for the time being. The gang was here in Coopersville, while Dan was at least a two-day's ride from here.

The bigger danger was to Tonto, though the Ranger wasn't certain whether they would want to kill him outright or use him as a wedge somehow. They might try to take him. But Tonto would not be easy to take. Outlaws had tried, only to find themselves in the hands of the law, facing a necktie party.

The Ranger searched his memory, but pinpointing an enemy who might have a notion to get even for something personal and have the brains to employ it was problematic. Most owlhoots were cowards at heart, notoriously cocky. Big with words, they seldom had the balls to back up something as rash as trying to lure the Ranger into an obvious snare. They were ambushers, impulsive, reckless. Not planners…

This gang leader was cut from different cloth. He had a reason behind his actions and a method to his madness. Again the word "personal" struck him. He had too many enemies to count, virtually every killer, robber and rustler west of the Mississippi, but how many of those were on a personal level? Very few, he thought. Most who would have reason to make a close kill were dead or in jail. Of those who weren't or had escaped, the percentage of them would not operate in such a progressive method. They were far more like to try a surprise attack, assassinate him out on the open trail.

Cavendish. The name rose in his mind again. He was such a man. An outlaw smart enough to plan in detail, resort to whatever means suited the situation, whether ambush or stealth. And he would have reason

72

for a personal vendetta. Yet, Butch Cavendish was dead. The Ranger had watched him die.

That left him with no suspects, yet the undeniable fact that somebody wanted vengeance and knew his identity, and was going about systematically implementing a plan to make certain their goal was accomplished.

"The foreman, Brent," Tonto said, eyes squinting against the afternoon sun. "He said the gang had taken over this town. But I see no one."

The Lone Ranger's gaze studied the empty street, then lifted to the rooftops in search of lookouts or snipers.

"Strange," he said. "I've seen towns taken over by outlaws before, lawless. They weren't this…quiet."

"A trap, Kemosabe?"

The Lone Ranger shook his head. "If it were it would have been sprung by now. We would have met some sort of resistance."

"Perhaps someone is waiting, watching."

Again the Ranger's gaze fanned out, studying each window, searching behind barrels and into alleyways for signs of life."

"If they are, they're being damn clever about it."

"Perhaps we should visit the marshal?" Tonto said. "Brent said he was one of the gang."

The Lone Ranger considered it, but confronting a gang member right off might be more direct than he wanted until he got a better handle on things. Until he knew better who he was dealing with, he preferred to scout around a bit, employ a subtle approach, since their open entry into town had drawn no immediate attention.

"We'll wait, Tonto, go after him if we can't learn more about this gang leader and his plan first."

Tonto's face hardened into grim lines. "I do not think we will have to wait long before this leader makes a move. He is getting a look at you, taking your measure."

"I have a notion he already had my measure before luring us here."

"You are the stuff of legend, Kemosabe. Words from writers of dime novels to most. Often those words are more than the men they describe. You are being judged worthy. By riding in without fear…you have confirmed the words of those writers to this leader."

The Ranger glanced at Tonto, a wry smile drifting onto his lips. "Always something to live up to…"

Tonto nodded. "In this case the man exceeds the legend. The leader will take no chances, now."

"The leader might not take chances, but one thing I've learned from years of experience bringing in owlhoots, you put more than one of them together and they get cocky and unruly. Only man I ever saw capable of preventing that was Cavendish, and men like him came along once in a blue moon."

A man came out of the bank onto the boardwalk ahead and the Ranger and Tonto's gazes swung in that direction. The man froze, fright welding onto his features, and he quickly shoved an envelope into his pocket, then spun. His boots echoed like gunshots as he bolted down the boardwalk and vanished around a corner.

"He thinks we're outlaws," the Lone Ranger said.

"I saw fright on his face, even before he saw us."

The Ranger nodded. "Brent was right. The people in this town are dead afraid. They are not venturing out and that makes this leader even more dangerous. It takes a lot to instill that kind of terror in an entire town."

"A lot…" Tonto muttered as a dark cloud drifted across his face and his arm came up, index finger stabbing toward a parked wagon a fifty feet on.

A chill snaked down the Lone Ranger's spine, despite the oppressive heat of the day. Bodies were stacked in the back of the wagon, at least six. Flies buzzed around the corpses and the stench of decay reached his nostrils.

"Good God…" The Ranger's voice came out a whisper.

"A reminder to anyone who might seek to oppose them," Tonto said. "This leader kills without compunction."

The Ranger nodded, forcing his gaze from the grisly sight. Ahead to the left, he saw the general store and again his blood went cold. Secured with ropes to a supporting beam of a wooden awning, was a saloon girl, partially clothed, wholly dead. Her arms had been tied above her head and she appeared to have been left like some sort of gruesome scarecrow.

"The leader left that there for us, Kemosabe. It is a warning."

"Inclined to agree," he said, slowing Silver and urging the great white stallion into an alley beside the store. Swallowing hard against the sight of that girl's body in his mind, he dismounted, Tonto drawing up beside him and doing the same. The Ranger removed a rolled blanket from his saddle, then walked to the front of the store to the body. Tonto withdrew the Bowie knife sheathed at his calf and cut the girl down. The Ranger caught her, lowered her to the boardwalk, then draped the blanket over her form. Frowning, he glanced at Tonto. The Indian's face was dark, his eyes hard.

Without words they went to the door of the general store. Tonto, who had sheathed his knife, tried the handle.

"Unlocked," he said, pushing the door inward.

"We're expected." The Ranger stepped inside. In the afternoon gloom, the interior carried an air of death. His gaze went to each aisle, spotted no one.

"Appears deserted," he said, moving deeper into the store. His attention settled on the wall behind the counter, on a splash of dried brown that smeared down the wall. He went to it, peered at the floor, where a dried brown patch stained the floorboards.

"I recollect Dan and I spending many a meal at Sanders' home. His wife could out cook nearly anyone in Texas." Sadness hung in the Ranger's voice. The thought of Sanders dead sent a wave of grief shuddering through him.

Tonto came around the counter, his dark eyes sympathetic. "There has been much death in this place. It will never be the same."

The Ranger sighed. "His body might have been one of those in the wagon. It'll need burying. Not much else I can do for him, now."

"There will be time for that, Kemosabe. But first

76

we must find his killer." Tonto knelt, his gaze going to a spot against the counter. He plucked a small object from the corner, stood.

The Ranger took it as the Indian held it up, frowning. "Another copper bullet."

"Someone is mocking you, Kemosabe."

"Got that right, Injun," a voice came from the doorway. The voice was accompanied by the *skritch* of a hammer being drawn back.

"S'pose you jest come around that counter nice and slowlike, Masked Man," the man standing in the doorway of the general store said, motioning with his gun. The man wore a tin star, but it was plain he was no real lawman. His eyes lacked the intelligence and compassion for the job and the Lone Ranger would have spotted the fake even had he not known of Marshal Moore's death. Beside the marshal, stood another man, plainly an outlaw, wearing a deputy's badge. His gun was trained on Tonto, hand shaking. That was bad. A nervous man made mistakes and folks got dead at the slightest provocation.

"You're no marshal," the Lone Ranger said, setting the copper bullet on the countertop and easing around to the front. He noticed the marshal's gun was trained on Tonto as well, though the man was doing his best to try to disguise that fact. There was a reason for that and the Lone Ranger didn't like it. It confirmed his earlier suspicions.

"Well, course I am," the man said, using bravado to cover the nervousness in his voice. He was antsy, too, like the deputy, but more experienced at hiding it. "This here star says so, don't it, Beemer?"

The deputy's head bobbed in affirmation and his gun hand jittered.

The Lone Ranger stepped left, making the move slow and easy, putting himself between Tonto and the deputy's line of fire. The expression that crossed the fake marshal's face confirmed the Ranger's notion—they had been given orders not to kill him immediately, but Tonto was another matter. If an accident happened, it happened.

"What do you want from us?" the Lone Ranger asked.

The marshal stepped deeper into the store, seeking to angle his aim around the Masked Man and place it back on the Indian.

"You and your Injun pal here are wanted for murder, ain't that right, Beemer?" Beemer nodded like some kind of puppet manipulated to respond to everything its master ordered.

"We did not murder anyone," Tonto said. He had not moved and the Ranger knew he had figured out the risk was greater for him.

"That so, Injun?" the marshal said. "I beg to differ. Got the body of a young gal lyin' right out there on the boardwalk that says different. Even got your blanket over her. Got witnesses who saw you with her out there, too."

"What witnesses?" the Ranger asked, knowing it made no difference, but seeking to stall. He edged forward a step, closing the distance between the two to five feet. The marshal gestured with his gun, stopping him from getting any closer.

"Beemer here saw you kill her, didn't you, Beemer?"

Beemer nodded again, shifted feet, his level of jitteriness notching upward. The deputy swallowed, his Adam's apple bobbing. The Ranger didn't like the way the man's finger twitched on the trigger. Not much was keeping him from accidentally blasting a shot.

"Why, it's plain to see you're an outlaw," the fake marshal said. "Wearin' a mask and everything. Why don't you just take it off and show us your face."

"Last person who saw my face took that sight with him to the grave," the Ranger said. "Man by the name of Butch Cavendish."

The name plainly startled the fake lawman. His eyes widened and he silently mouthed the name. The reaction puzzled the Ranger, but he took advantage of it. The outlaw's hesitation was his opportunity. His hand swept to his Peacemakers and the guns came from their holsters in a blur of motion. It was a risk, but a calculated one. Both men were not expecting immediate resistance.

Two shots thundered in the confines of the store. Silver bullets drilled into the gunhand of each man.

The deputy let out a shriek as his weapon flew from his grip and hit the floor a half-dozen feet away. Blood dripped from his hand. Panic flashed across his face and he dove for the weapon.

Tonto sprang to the countertop with the Ranger's draw. He launched himself into space toward the diving deputy, landed in front of the man. The deputy tried to stop, throw a punch. Tonto's arm came up, deflected the blow. The Indian snapped a short hook into the deputy's ribs, spun and followed up with a kick to the chest that sent the man stumbling backward.

On instinct, the deputy snatched a bag of flour

from a stack piled next to the shelf, hoisted it, intending to hurl it at the charging Indian.

Tonto doubled, hand sweeping for his knife, straightened again. The blade flashed up, sliced a path through the sack. Flour exploded in a great billowing cloud, coating Tonto and the deputy poised to throw the sack.

The Indian pivoted, planted a foot in the deputy's middle. The man hurtled backward, still holding the spewing sack, and crashed into a shelf piled with canned goods. He collapsed, the cans raining atop him.

To Tonto's left, the Ranger spun his guns on his index fingers and jammed them back into their holsters. The bullet had sent the marshal's pistol skidding out the open shop door and the outlaw stood clutching his mangled hand.

The Lone Ranger pistoned a fist straight into the man's face. With a spray of blood, the marshal's nose turned into pulpy mass.

The fake lawman was tough; the Ranger had to give him that much. Despite the fact his hand and face were damaged, he swung a roundhouse left that might have taken off the Ranger's head had it landed.

The Ranger doubled and the blow whisked over his head. He snapped back upright, launching an uppercut that crashed into the lawdog's chin that lifted him clean off the floor. The marshal hurtled over a pickle barrel, the barrel toppling over with him, splashing him and floor with brine. He lay there, groaning, uneager to resume the fight.

The Ranger swung his gaze to Tonto, who stood there half-covered with flour.

81

"You look like a white man," he said, a slight smile quirking his lips.

"Urm, Kemosabe speak with forked tongue."

"Someone will have heard the shots. We need to go."

They left the store, the Ranger first casting a cautious look about. He saw no one, but had the sudden impression they were being watched.

They ran for the alley and their horses. Mounting, he pulled on the reins and slapped his heels against the great horse's sides.

"Hi-yo, Silver!" he yelled and the stallion bolted from the alley, Tonto close on his heels.

#

She walked into the general store after the Ranger and his savage had left, her gaze taking in the overturned barrel, coating of flour that lay over the floorboards like fresh snow, and her two men. Pathetic sights, they were, each bloodied and struggling to get to their feet. She had half a mind to shoot them and leave them there.

"'Bout what I expected," she said, stepping over to a spot near the shelf and retrieving a mangled bullet that lay there. She peered at it, a cold expression on her face. Silver. The Ranger's bullet. She went to the counter, set the silver bullet next to the copper one lying there, then turned back to her men.

"You're gawdamned lucky I ain't got immediate replacements for you two peckerwoods."

The fake marshal and deputy glanced at each other.

"He was tougher than we thought," the marshal

82

said, as if it made a difference.

She made a scoffing sound. "Of course he was. You were s'posed to get that Injun. I need him."

"We tried," the deputy said, on obvious trembling now gripping his entire body. It was plain the memory of her killing that dove earlier this morning was still fresh in his mind. She almost laughed. He wasn't long for this gang. Neither was the other, but for now she couldn't afford the loss of any more men.

"You best see to it the next time I give you a job you do it right."

Both men nodded, clearly relieved they hadn't swallowed lead pills.

"Get cleaned up. I want that Injun. I've seen enough of the Ranger to know what they write about him ain't exaggerated. I reckoned he had to be something special to get Butch; wasn't dumb luck after all."

"How?" the marshal asked. "Ain't never seen anyone draw that fast."

She uttered a lifeless laugh. "Won't be long 'fore he comes back. He'll want to learn more about me and will be a lot more crafty about it next time. They'll separate. The Injun backs him up. When that happens…you best have a plan, 'less you got a notion to retire early."

14

"Whoever we're dealing with is going to step up their plan now that they got a look at us in action," the Lone Ranger said, gazing out at the stream that looked like black glass frosted with wavering ribbons of alabaster under the moonlit sky. They'd set up camp a short distance from town, near a stream flanked by boulders and scrub pine. They night was still pleasant and he forewent the luxury of a fire, not wanting to alert the gang as to just where they had holed up. He doubted the leader would attack them outright, but saw no need to take chances.

"Those men…their guns were aimed at me, not you, Kemosabe," Tonto said. "They want you alive."

The Lone Ranger nodded. "For the moment. We're going to have to be more careful, now. I want a parley with that fake marshal, and next time it'll be on my terms, but for now he can wait. The gang is holed up somewhere in town; I have a notion it's somewhere in plain sight."

"The saloon?"

"A good possibility. And if anyone would know, it'd be the barkeep or one of the line girls. I need to question them."

"If they're as frightened as the rest of the town, they will not talk freely."

With a sigh, the Ranger folded his arms and his eyes narrowed on the flowing stream water. "No, they won't. And if the gang is using the place as a head-quarters, that will make it even less likely one of them will dare say something."

"Especially to the Lone Ranger."

"I have to try. I can't wait for them to kill more innocent people."

"How?" Tonto's brow furrowed. "You cannot just walk in there. If the gang is using the place, they will have men posted in the saloon, to intimidate the towns-folk. The leader might not want you dead immediately, but he will take you if he has the chance."

The Ranger nodded. "The thought occurred to me. If that fake marshal had put us in a cell, this would be over by now."

"I can sneak in the back, Kemosabe. If they have Cooper there, perhaps I can free him."

"The leader will suspect we'll make a move on Cooper and be ready for it—unless I divert his attention. Questioning the 'keep and some of the girls might just serve a dual purpose, information on the gang if they are holed up there or close by, and creating a diversion."

The Ranger, unfolded his arms, walked over to Silver, who was tethered loosely to a low scrub branch next to Scout.

"You plan to walk right in there?" A look of disapproval mixed with concern crossed Tonto's face.

The Lone Ranger grabbed his saddlebags, swung them over a shoulder and glanced back at the Indian, giving him a slight smile. "No, I don't. But Gabby does…"

An hour later an old man staggered down the boardwalk toward the saloon. A worn poncho, too big for his frame, hung to his knees, tangled there, and nearly sent him sprawling to the boardwalk. He let out a string of muttered curses and righted himself, kept onward. A gray beard touched the top of his chest and straggly gray hair flowed from beneath a low-pulled battered hat with a too-wide brim. Dark circles nested beneath his eyes and deep-set wrinkles spider-webbed from around his mouth. His skin had a ruddy scrubbed complexion that spoke of many a day in the blazing sunlight and many a night under the cold stars. He hunched as he walked, taking inches off what probably was his true height when he stood straight. He appeared a prospector who had seen better days and had taken to the bottle to wait out his remaining ones.

A song suddenly tumbled from his lips, coming at the top of his voice, an old mining ditty as worn as the man himself. Few were out to hear it. He noticed a marshal standing outside his office, smoking a rolled cigarette and giving him a curious eye. The marshal's hand was bandaged and livid bruises formed half circles beneath his eyes. After studying him for a moment, the lawman appeared to decide the prospector posed no threat and flicked his cigarette toward the old one.

"Picked the wrong town to come into jest now, you dirty old bastard," the marshal said, a vicious expression washing across his face. "You best leave."

The old prospector stopped his song, mumbled something uncomplimentary about the lawman's line-

86

age, and spat at the boardwalk.

Anger reddened the marshal's face and his hand slipped to his gun. It paused there, and he muttered a *pfft* of a sound, made a vulgar gesture, then turned and went back into his office.

"Oh, Susanna, don't you cry fer me!" the prospector sang again, and resumed his stumbling course toward the saloon.

When he reached the saloon, he stopped, clamped his mouth shut, and cast a causal glance about him, as if he were merely half in his cups and his actions aimless. From within the saloon the sounds of a tinkler piano banging off key floated out into the night, along with a smattering of curses and rowdy laughter.

He pushed through the batwings, paused just inside on the short landing that led to the barroom proper. The scene might have been that in any of a hundred such establishments scattered across the West. An iron-wheel chandelier hung in the center of the barroom and a stairway rising to the upper rooms where the doves plied their trade flanked the south wall. A mezzanine hallway ran the length of the back, disappearing into a hallway beyond. A number of cowboys from local ranches sat around green-felted tables playing poker, chuck-a-luck or sliding cards from a tiger-emblazoned box in a game called Faro. Rotgut whiskey flowed freely and saloon girls in sateen bodices and peek-a-boo blouses leaned over the shoulders of winners, exhibiting generous portions of their bosoms and giggling wooden nickel giggles, or whispering of secret promises for a dollar a turn.

The scene came through a layer of Durham smoke,

and the stench of old vomit, cheap booze and even cheaper perfume applied far too liberally assailed the old prospector's nostrils, but it made no difference to him.

Despite the frivolity of the atmosphere, a subdued feeling of somberness permeated the saloon. It was palpable, like a threat, and many of the cowboys seemed antsy, the saloon girls more so.

One man did not appear to share that feeling. He sat at a table, whiskey glass in hand and bottle before him. A bardove sat on his lap, her face tense as his free hand fondled her breast. His features showed he was enjoying the situation a great deal, and he peered at the old man through glazed eyes, half-closed. He wore the look of a cat in a room full of mice.

The old prospector didn't linger on the landing for long. He took the three steps to the saloon floor, nearly tumbling down them in the process, which elicited a vacant laugh from the man with the dove sitting on his lap. The old man brushed at his arms, as if dust had fallen onto his poncho, and the man with the whore raised a whiskey glass to him, the look on his face saying he thought the old one was clearly loco and it was a hell of a funny thing.

The old man's boots hit the sawdust-covered floor as if he'd expected another step to be there, then he weaved his way through the tables toward the bar. The tinkler began playing "Silver Threads Among the Gold," adding wrong notes, but no one in the room appeared to care. The player was nervous, fingers missing keys, not unskilled. His hands shook and the old prospector frowned a bit.

As he reached the bar, he pulled out a stool and managed to get himself onto it after nearly tumbling off on the first attempt. A redheaded saloon girl leaning on the far end of the bar cast him a look that said he was no prospect, then ignored him.

"What's your poison, gent?" the barkeep asked, wiping out the glass in his hand. He set the glass on the counter before the old man.

The old man's head lifted, briefly focused on his reflection in a big gilded mirror behind the bar between two hutches stocked with bottles. He was a sight, that was for sure, he thought.

"Whiskey," the old man said, and the bartender grabbed a bottle from the hutch. He poured two fingers, capped the bottle.

"Two bits," the barman said, little expression in his voice, but a measure of fear in his eyes.

The prospector dug in a pocket of his poncho, brought out an object and slapped it on the bartop, then pulled his trembling hand away.

The 'keep stared at the object, and the fear in his eyes became a wounded animal. His tongue flicked over chapped lips and his Adam's apple bobbed.

"What's wrong with ya, son?" the old man asked, eyes suddenly intense. "Ya never seen silver bullet before? Make them from my own mine, I do."

The barkeep snatched up the bullet, as if wanting to make certain no one got a look at it. He cast a sideways glance towards the man with the bardove in his lap, then looked back to the prospector.

"Who are you?" the 'keep asked, voice low, with a hint of a tremble.

"Why, name's Gabby," the old man said. "Yep, indeedy, it is. Come down from Colorada way after seekin' my fortune in silver and gold. Figgered on doin' me some prospectin' 'round these parts."

"There's no gold here…" The barkeep cast another glance at the man with the bargirl.

"I'm not prospectin' for gold…" the old man said, not making a move to pick up the whiskey glass. His hand dipped into his pocket a second time, this time coming out with a double eagle and setting it on the counter.

The 'keep peered at the coin, greed nearly overriding the fear in his demeanor. "What are you prospectin' for?"

"Information." The old man's voice had steadied, and any sign of dullness had vanished from his eyes. They now appeared intelligent and probing.

"You'll get us all killed, whoever you are." The 'keep's voice dropped to a whisper and the fear returned, stronger.

"That man behind me," the prospector said, ignoring the barman's words, his own voice now sounding much younger than his appearance. "A hardcase. Who does he work for and where is the leader?"

"Please…" the 'keep said, a plea haunting his voice. "Just go. Leave us be. They'll leave soon. They have to. Outlaws always do."

"They generally leave after a lot of death. You want more of that on your conscience?" The old man's eyes drilled the barkeep and the man flinched under their gaze.

"It's not my fault. I just want to mind my business

and live my life."

"Enough men thought like that the West would be run by lunatics."

"Ain't it?" the 'keep said. "What's the difference to you?"

"It's the difference between humanity and the likes of his type. Who's leadin' them and where is this man?"

"Ain't a man…" the 'keep said, then clamped his mouth shut. He swallowed hard, backed up a step. "Oh, Christ…"

A hand fell on the prospector's shoulder, landing with a degree of force calculated to cause pain to one as aged as the man appeared. The prospector shuddered, winced, his head swiveling.

"Son, I'm an old man. What you gotta go hurt me fer?"

The hardcase peered at the old man, and if he had been a bit more sober it might have been over right there. Makeup only went so far to hide a young face.

"You're takin' up a lot of the man's time," the hardcase said, voice cold. "Best drink up and be on your way 'fore my boss comes along."

"Who might your boss be, gent?" The prospector yanked his shoulder free, rubbed it.

"You knew the answer to that you'd be leavin' in the back of a wagon. Boss don't like newcomers in this town, especially those who ask too many questions."

"Jest makin' conversation, son. And I ain't leavin' till I'm durn good and ready."

The man stared at him as if surprised the old one had defied the order. Then he grabbed the prospector and hurled him off the stool.

91

The old man stumbled, almost going down, only righting himself at the last moment. He made a brushing motion at both arms again, cursed under his breath.

"Told you to leave, old man. You best pay attention."

"And I told ya ta go to the Devil."

Without warning, the hardcase swung a fist. Even so, the old man could have gotten out of its way, for the punch was sloppy, targeted at someone who had no chance of escaping it. But he didn't. He took it, jerking his head just enough at the last moment to lessen the effects of the blow. Still, he went backwards and down, hitting the floor of his rump in a cloud of sawdust. He swiped at a dribble of blood that came from his lip.

The hardcase froze, shock crossing his features, sobering him. "Oh, Christ on a crutch..." he muttered, gaze fixed on the old man.

The prospector didn't know what had given it away for an instant, then he saw it. His poncho had come up in the fall, revealing an ivory-handled .45 at the old man's right hip.

"You should be more careful who you're hitting," the old man said, voice now young, vibrant. He whipped the hat off his head. The gray wig came with it. He started to rise.

The hardcase let out a startled gasp and grabbed a table, hurled it over onto the old man and ran. He weaved through the sea of tables, aiming for the staircase at the back of the room.

The old man flung the table away and came to his feet. He shucked off the poncho, tossed it aside, revealing both .45s in holsters about his waist.

The tinkler had gone silent and cowboys and bar-girls backed out of the way, fear on their faces. The Ranger couldn't blame them; they had seen enough death in the last few days and wanted no part of riling up the outlaws who'd delivered it. He did not have that option. He'd gotten what he came for and he hoped Tonto was having success sneaking into the back of the saloon. Regardless, he could not let the hardcase stumble across the Indian upstairs.

The outlaw had made it to the top of the stairs. He drew his gun, fired a shot down into the saloon, but had taken no time to aim. The bullet buried itself in a floor-board and a bargirl shrieked.

The Ranger lunged into motion, leaping to a chair, then propelling himself to a table top and launching himself into the air. Up he went, his hands stabbing out, catching the far edge of the iron chandelier, swinging, his feet whipping up before him. He let go at the exact instant his heels came up over his head and momen-tum carried him up and over the mezzanine rail. He landed hard, in a crouch. The hardcase swept a back-ward look, fired again, but the bullet went far wide.

The outlaw bolted down a red foil-papered hall-way. Buttery light from a low-turned wall lantern barely illuminated the hall.

The Ranger came after him, gaining. His hand went to a .45, snatched it from its holster. He fired a shot ahead, aiming wide, not seeking to kill the man, merely slow him. But the hardcase, now panicked, poured on more speed.

The outlaw reached the end of the hall and a win-dow there that led to an outside staircase. He thrust the window up faster than the Ranger would have thought possible, and a swung leg over the sill before the Ranger made it halfway down the hall. An instant later, the hardcase disappeared outside.

As the Ranger reached the window, he paused, not eager to eat a bullet if the outlaw was waiting for him. He glanced back into the hallway, at the rows of doors to either side, wandering if Tonto was in one of the rooms. He didn't have time to check. If he did he would lose the man, and a possible lead to the gang leader.

The Lone Ranger eased his head through the window, prepared to instantly draw it back if the hardcase was lying in wait for him. He glimpsed the man scrambling up the stairs, reaching the top and leaping to grip the edge of the roof.

The Ranger went through the window, gun in hand. The top was only a flight up and he took the stairs in seconds, momentarily holstered his gun and leaped, catching the edge of the roof. He hoisted himself up, flung a leg over and tumbled onto the flat roof. He kept rolling, drawing his gun again, ready to fire if the hardcase tried a shot at him.

But the man didn't. He bolted along the roof, reaching the opposite edge behind the false front that extended above roof level. Once there, he spun, triggered a shot. Lead whined past the Ranger's ear and he crouched low, firing back. He had hoped to hit the man's gunhand but in the poor light it was an almost impossible shot.

The hardcase fired again, and this time the shot went wider. The man was scared, taking no time to aim. The Ranger triggered another, too, and the man staggered as silver punched into his shoulder.

The hardcase tried to lift his gun but his arm appeared crippled from the Ranger's shoulder hit. The gun dropped from his fingers and the outlaw cursed, whirled.

"No!" the Ranger yelled, lunging forward as the man hopped to the lip of the roof and launched himself into space towards the next roof. It wasn't much of a jump, but panic had caused him to misjudge it. He hit the side of the next building, tried to grab at the top, using one arm. His fingertips caught the lip, but couldn't hold on. He dropped, and a heavy thud came a second later.

The Ranger halted near the edge, holstered his gun. A frown pulled at his lips as he peered over the edge and saw the twisted body lying in the hardpack below.

15

Tonto kept to the shadows as he skirted the smaller back street running parallel to the wide main one. His moccasined feet seemed to barely touch the ground as he moved, and only the occasional rustle of buckskin marked his passage. Anyone hearing it would have thought it the breeze.

This man who led the Blood Creek Gang was brutal, perhaps more brutal as Butch Cavendish had ever been. He killed without compunction, and was, as all outlaws were, a coward at heart. He would not face the Ranger man to man; he would trap him, use a bait the Masked Man could not resist, then kill him once he was helpless. Tonto knew too well what that bait had to be, himself or young Dan. That meant he had to be more alert than he had ever been, as the rabbit is alert for the shadow of the hawk, and that they had to bring this gang to ground before they tracked down the Ranger's nephew.

He would not let this leader trap Kemosabe, especially by using him, even if it meant forfeiting his own life. Either would have gladly given his life for the other, and Tonto was prepared to sacrifice whatever it took to ensure the Ranger's mission went on. It was too important. The West held too many men willing to kill and steal, rape and hurt, but only one man willing to give up all to protect the innocent.

A grim expression welded to the Indian's lips. It was perversely ironic in a way. This man who led the gang, he had viciously murdered many to get to one man, and it was his type who called Tonto's race savage. Without Kemosabe and men like him, Tonto doubted the West had much hope.

A clamor sounded from the front street and Tonto paused, ears pricked. Singing, loud and off key. Kemosabe might have been a man blessed with many skills, but carrying a tune was not one of them.

Tonto moved ahead again, the Lone Ranger by his boisterous song having given him the signal he was close to the saloon and would enter within a few moments. He pressed himself close to the walls of buildings, slipped towards an alley ahead that flanked the saloon. Reaching the edge of a building he waited until the Ranger's singing stopped, telling him he was entering the saloon. He would wait another moment, give the Ranger time in case something went wrong and the plan for Tonto to sneak up into the saloon needed to be aborted. Even if some of the gang were in the saloon, there would be guards around Cooper if he were being held prisoner in one of the rooms above. If not, the rooms would be empty, with the possible exception of whores tending to the needs of gang members. Either way, no one would hear him coming.

He started to move around into the alley, suddenly stopped as a voice reached his ears.

"Don't see what we gotta do it out here for," a

voice said. The voice belonged to a woman and held fear.

"'Cause if she catches me with you I'll end up like that idjit, Trent," a male's voice returned, tone brooking no argument. "She's gone and made me her favorite."

Tonto's brow furrowed. He didn't recognize the name Trent or understand quite what the man was referring to, or who this "she" might be, but his instinct told him the man belonged to the gang. He edged his head around the corner, peered into the alley. Wan moonlight penetrated the passage, which was stacked with old crates and barrels, littered with garbage from the saloon, old beefsteak and chicken bones. Two people were in the alley, a man and a woman. The woman was jammed up against the building wall, her hard face tense with fear. She was dressed in a blue sateen bodice and frilly skirt—one of the saloon girls.

The man had his back partially to him, his face pressed close to the girl's, his hands holding both her upper arms, fingers gouging in. A hardcase, and Tonto felt certain his conclusion of a moment before, that this man was part of the gang, was correct. The problem now became how to get into the saloon. An outside staircase ran up the opposite side of the place, but he had decided against using it in case guards were posted at the window it accessed. On this side, he could stack the crates and barrels and climb up to look through a window leading into one of the rooms, but these two were in the way and if he guessed correctly about what the man wanted from the girl, they would be there for more time than Tonto cared to wait.

The problem complicated itself an instant later. The man let go of the girl, backhanded her with an explosive violence that made Tonto's teeth clench. The girl let out a bleat and her head rocked. She slumped but the man caught her, held her up.

"P-please…" the girl said, the fear in her voice heavier now.

The man laughed, a mocking unsympathetic sound that burned like fire through Tonto's mind. Balls of muscles stood out on either side of his jaw and his teeth started to ache from clenching.

"What's wrong, you stupid whore?" the man said, then jammed his lips to hers. He pulled back, laughing again. "Don't you know it's better rough? She taught me that, missy. Showed me how pain and pleasure went together." He slammed the girl against the wall; her body shuddered, her ringlets of blonde hair coming loose from a silk red ribbon she'd used to tie them up.

The man was going to kill the girl, if he kept it up. She appeared stunned, had hit her head against the wall. The hardcase was forced to hold her with one hand. His other balled into a fist and he cocked his arm in preparation for another blow.

Tonto debated drawing his gun, shooting the man, but Kemosabe's code against killing stopped him. And if he could take this man alive, perhaps the mission would not be for nothing. They could made him talk, tell them where Cooper was being held and who led this gang.

Tonto glided forward, giving it no more thought. His steps were silent as he approached the hardcase.

The man's hand came up a fraction more then

started down. His fist would crash into her face and whether she survived it or not the man would take her afterward.

The thought sickened Tonto. His hand shot out, clamped about the wrist of the hardcase, stopping his blow before it came halfway down.

"What the hell?" the man blurted, his head swinging around, eyes wide, half glazed by whiskey. His face held a number of scratches, a day or two old, marred his face and fury raged across his features.

"You no hit woman," Tonto said, slipping into the speech white men expected from an Indian. Tonto had used that speech many times to his advantage, as protective technique to take outlaws off guard.

"Goddammit, an Injun!" the man said, as if he couldn't believe what he was seeing. "Where the goddamn hell didchu come from?" The hardcase tried to jerk his hand free but Tonto held it fast, fingers tightening.

"You leave woman be," Tonto said, dark eyes narrowing.

The man let her be. He released his grip on her and she slumped to the ground, looking up, dazed, at the two men.

"What's wrong, Injun? I thought all you redskins treated your women like property. Trade 'em off for horses, doncha? Have yourself more than one at a time, I hear." The man's free hand was moving down toward his gun as he spoke, trying to distract the Indian. It was an old ploy and Tonto was ready for it.

Tonto let go of his wrist, brought his knee up and buried it in the man's groin. The hardcase doubled, making gagging sounds.

The bargirl stared screaming. The sound was shrill and raked Tonto's ears, startling him, it came so unexpectedly.

"No, you no scream, missy. Me help you." He didn't know if the sound would carry into the saloon over the din, but it no longer mattered because a shot came from the barroom and the girl's mouth clamped shut. With a glance Tonto could tell the terror had gotten the better of her and she had blacked out. The blow to the back of her head against the wall had probably helped.

The Indian's teeth gritted. Any chance of sneaking into the upper rooms of the saloon was over. His only saving grace was taking the man doubled over and groaning before him back to camp and questioning him, assuming Kemosabe escaped whatever trouble was happening in the saloon.

The hardcase had other ideas. He reared up, wrapped both arms around Tonto's waist and lurched, carrying the Indian backwards into a stack of crates. The crates gave, the breaking wood sounding like snapping bones. They tumbled down about the two. Tonto hit the ground on his rear, arm flung up to keep any of the crates from hitting his head. If he wound up incapacitated at all the hardcase would kill him.

He came up, half to his feet when a fist crashed into his jaw. He staggered, almost going down again, the world spinning before him. On instinct he lifted an arm, deflecting a second blow aimed at his temple.

Shaking his head, Tonto swung an uppercut, hoping to get lucky. The blow skimmed the hardcase's face, knocking him off balance but doing little damage.

101

"Don't think I know who you are, do ya, Injun?" the hardcase said, his voice raspy. "You're with the god-damn Ranger she wants so bad. Reckon I give you to her she'll leave me the hell alone."

The world stopped spinning before Tonto's eyes. The hardcase was going for his gun again. He got his hand on it, lifted it half out of the holster.

Tonto grabbed for the man's wrist, got it, but the Smith & Wesson came free. The hardcase was strong, but the Indian was stronger. He forced the gun's aim away from him.

A blow stung the side of his head as the outlaw hammered a fist into Tonto's temple, and again the shadows and moonlight of the alley streaked before his vision. It stopped quickly this time and the Indian shoved forward, carrying the hardcase backward. They hit the wall of the opposite building hard, Tonto's hand still clamped around the other's wrist.

The hardcase shuddered and the Smith & Wesson went off, as his finger spasmed on the trigger. For an in-stant Tonto wasn't sure where the bullet had hit. Then the outlaw crumpled against the wall. Tonto let go of his wrist and the gun dropped from the man's nerve-less fingers.

He knelt, examining the man. Blood shined black under the moonlight, pumping from the man's ab-domen. The man's mouth moved, but no sound came out, then he went silent, his head dropping to his chest.

Tonto felt the man's wrist, found no pulse. He would not be taking this man back to camp for ques-tioning. The outlaw was dead.

He grabbed the outlaw's legs and stood, dragged

him into the shadows, disgusted with himself. He had come away empty handed.

Somewhere above him more shots rang out. His gaze lifted, but he saw nothing. Someone was on the roof, two someones; that was the most he could tell.

He went to the bargirl, bent over her and lightly patted her face. She stirred, her eyes coming open.

"Me friend. You tell me what happens in saloon."

She shook her head, panic flashing across her face as her senses returned. "No, no, I can't! They'll kill me."

Tonto helped the woman to her feet. "What name?" he asked.

"Tilly," she said.

"Tilly, me…" Tonto suddenly abandoned the Indian speak, gripped her shoulders. He needed to instill confidence in this girl and playing the part of an ignorant savage would not do it. "I have a friend. He will protect you."

She stared at him, as if puzzled why he had suddenly changed his speech pattern. "No one can help. They'll kill us all!"

A crash came from above and Tonto swept the girl back into the shadows, as his gaze lifted. A man slammed into the opposite building wall, then fell to the ground with a heavy thud. From the twisted position of his neck, Tonto could tell he would not be getting up again. The girl stared, her mouth moving but no sound coming out.

He propped her against the wall, then went to the body, knelt. The man was a hardcase. His shoulder was bloody from a bullet wound.

103

Tonto stood, and footsteps came from the far end of the alley. The Lone Ranger, sporting the gray beard still, came into the alley, gun drawn.

"This one is not my fault," Tonto said, as the Ranger came up to him.

"There's another?" the Ranger asked.

Tonto nodded. "It was an accident."

The bargirl apparently had had all she could take for the night because she suddenly started shrieking again and bolted from the alley.

Tonto frowned. He had been hoping to get at least some information out of her once he gained her trust.

"Who was that?" the Ranger asked, beckoning Tonto to follow him from the alley.

"Tilly," Tonto said, offering no further information.

"Tilly?" the Ranger said. "Care to elaborate?"

"No," Tonto said, annoyed with himself at the way events had turned out, then added: "I could not get into the saloon."

"I didn't get the chance to look into any of the rooms. They might have been empty or the leader could have been behind one of the doors."

Commotion came from the main street, likely the fake marshal and his deputy, neither too fast to investigate. Cowards.

"The gang is down two men, Kemosabe, but we don't know how many they came with."

"We'll leave for now, before the entire gang comes after us," the Ranger said, nodding. "But I want another look at the upstairs of that saloon."

#

An hour later, the door to the room the gang was

using came open behind her but she didn't turn from where she stood, gazing out the window into the moonlit night. Things had not gone well, and it displeased her. And when she was displeased someone got dead.

"What happened?" she asked, not turning to the hardcase posing as the marshal, who stood in the doorway. To her right Trace Cooper sat tied to a chair wearing only his underwear, his silk robe having been stripped from him and cut into strips with which to bind him to the chair and fashion a gag. His chin rested on his chest and his eyes, swollen and livid, were closed. Dried blood was caked on his fingertips where the nails had been pried off. Bruises, deep purple, covered his arms and face.

"Calvin's dead," the fake marshal said, stepping into the room and shutting the door behind him.

She laughed. "Good. The damn fool almost led the Ranger right up to me. I would have killed him myself. Can't abide by mistakes like that. I don't like the way this is going."

"I don't, either," Parker said. "The Ranger…many men have gone up against him and gotten a necktie party. Maybe we best—"

"No!" she said, spinning from the window, anger flashing across her face. "We're going nowhere until I have him. I won't tolerate any more mistakes, Parker. The Ranger came into the saloon alone. You find that gawdamn Injun and bring him to me."

"We searched the town, didn't find either of them."

Christ, she wanted to kill him just to get the tension out of her nerves, but he was the smartest of the bunch, which according to her estimation after tonight,

105

wasn't saying a hell of a lot.

"They'll try again. Be ready for them next time and keep your gawdamn eyes open."

Parker shifted feet, his face tight. "There's something else…"

"What?" she said, voice snapping like a whip.

"Matthews is dead, too. Found him shot in the alley next to the saloon. The Injun got him. One of the bargals came screeching out of the alley. I grabbed her, made her talk. She said an Injun saved her after Matthews started hittin' her."

She turned back to the window, fury running through her veins like wildfire. This was unacceptable. She was down to six men and had gotten nothing out of Cooper. One of her men had almost ruined her entire plan an hour ago and another was no longer alive for her to take her frustration out on.

"Kill her…" she said, voice icy.

"Ma'am?" Parker said, blinking.

"Kill that bargirl Matthews had. Fact, kill everybody in the saloon. The Ranger will learn his actions have consequences, severe ones."

"Everybody?" Parker said.

"Everybody."

16

The Lone Ranger arose with the dawn, his night a restless one, sleep coming in snatches filled with blood-splashed nightmares. Too much death had surrounded him throughout his mission. It seemed to follow him, stalk him. And the longer the leader of this gang was allowed to remain at large, taunting him, the more innocent blood he would feel responsible for. He had to stop him…him? What had the barkeep said last night?

He looked over at Tonto, who had set a blue enameled pot of Arbuckle's to brewing. With the morning light they could risk a small campfire.

"The 'keep last night," the Ranger said. "I've been over what he said in my mind a hundred times, searching for something that might lead me to the identity of this gang leader. He said 'Ain't a man', when I was asked who the leader was."

Tonto nodded, taking two tin cups from his saddle bag, then lifting the coffee pot from the fire. "The outlaw in the alley used the word, 'she'. This leader…appears be a woman."

"If it is, it still brings me no closer to a name."

"Perhaps this woman was associated with Cavendish, somehow. She operates in much the same way."

The Ranger considered it. It made sense. But as

far as he knew Cavendish had no relatives left alive.

"Time's run out. If Cooper is still alive he won't last much longer and if she sticks to pattern she'll go after you, then Dan, and soon."

"If they were using the saloon as a headquarters they will have likely abandoned it after last night and gone into hiding. Moved Cooper." Tonto poured two cups of coffee, handed one to the Ranger.

The Ranger nodded. "Unless they didn't need him anymore…" He took a sip of the coffee, letting its bitter warmth flow down his throat. "They lost two men, though we don't know how many are left. They'll be more careful. It's time to have a talk with that fake marshal. He's an open lead to the gang."

"Assuming he will even return to his office, now." Tonto paused. "I will search the saloon upstairs. Perhaps they left something behind."

The Ranger gave his friend a disapproving glance. He didn't like the idea of Tonto going alone, not when he was most likely the woman's next target. He knew the Indian could take care of himself, but a twinge of dread cinched his belly.

"If one of them should still be there…"

Tonto gave him a grim smile. "All the better. Or perhaps the bargirl from last night will talk if they are gone."

"I won't waste much time with the marshal if he is there, and join you at the saloon."

#

The Marshal looked nervous as he snuck through the back door of his office, too nervous to notice the lock had been jimmied. He went to a blue enameled coffee pot on a small table, poured cold coffee into a tin cup and gulped it down. A visible shudder traveled through his frame.

A wonder crossed the Lone Ranger's mind. Why *was* the man back in the office after last night? Was the gang leader, whoever she was, that cocky he and Tonto would not try to question the man, or was there another reason? He thought of Tonto sneaking into the saloon and the apprehension stalking his nerves increased. Something was wrong, as it had been on that day he and five other men had ridden into Bryant's Gap. And he had a notion he was playing right into it.

The marshal didn't move for a moment, then poured himself another cup. After, he pulled a flask from his pocket and added the contents to the coffee.

The Ranger watched him from a hardbacked chair just beyond the shaft of dusty early-morning light streaming in through the large front window, an ivory-handled .45 in his hand.

"I'm the one you should be afraid of..." he said, voice hard.

"Jesus!" The fake lawdog started, the cup jumping out of his hand and landing with a clink on the floor-boards. He whirled, hand going for his gun.

"Don't!" the Ranger said, coming out of the chair, gun leveled on the man. The lawdog apparently thought better of trying to draw, glanced at his bandaged hand. "Unbuckle your belt, let it drop."

The man hesitated and the Ranger gestured with his gun. Fingers going to his belt, the marshal undid the buckle; the belt along with his holstered Smith & Wesson fell to the floor.

"Over there." The Ranger indicated one of the cells in a bank of three at the rear of the office.

The marshal moved to the first cell, paused. "What do you want?"

"Who do you work for? Who is she?" The Ranger's voice came hard as tension built further within him. He glanced towards the window, in the direction of the saloon. Was he wasting time here?

"I ain't tellin' you nothin'," the marshal said, voice shaking.

"Maybe you don't have to. Because I'm asking myself, why are you here after last night? Why would your leader, who has planned so carefully to this point, leave you out in the open?"

The marshal shifted feet and a tick fired near his blackened eye. "What do you mean?"

The Ranger's eyes narrowed behind the half-mask, searching the man for the slightest betrayal of his mission. "Your leader…she's got the brains I think she does, she would figure out I'd go after the most obvious link to her gang. You're the sacrificial lamb, aren't you, Marshal?"

The marshal started again, his eyes betraying his thoughts. He'd been sent to detain the Ranger and didn't like the job one bit.

"Get in the cell," the Ranger said, gesturing again with his gun. He had a choice. Stay and try to get answers from this man as to where the gang was located or get to the saloon and Tonto before whatever plan the leader had in mind went into operation.

No. No choice, really. No choice at all.

The Ranger backed to the wall, where a peg held a

key ring, keeping his gun on the fake lawman as he did so. Keys in hand, the Ranger went to the door, locked it, then tossed the key ring across the room where the man would never be able to get to it.

Holstering his gun, he went out the back door, a sense of urgency quickening his steps and his heart as he headed for the saloon.

#

Though he had said nothing to Kemosabe, Tonto knew if the gang allowed the marshal to return to his office after last night's events, the man would say nothing about the identity of the gang leader. The fake lawman would be frightened of the Ranger, but Kemosabe's reputation for not killing would hurt him in this instance, because the gang leader had no such limitations and would certainly kill the man in cold blood if he told anything.

The Indian slipped along the back of the saloon, early morning sunlight chasing away shadows and heating the day. A quick look into the alley told him both bodies had been removed, but the crates were hopelessly smashed. He would have to use the outside staircase.

Every sense alert, Tonto worked his away around the building to the staircase. Things seemed too tranquil again. Had the gang ever been based in the saloon? Or were members just using the girls? Had Cooper been here? Or was he dead? He knew it would not take much of a search to determine those answers once he got inside, but he hoped he would discover some small clue to lead them to the gang's hideout.

He eased up the staircase, steps silent as a ghost's,

until he reached the second story window. Pressing himself to the building beside the window, he chanced a look into the gloomy hallway.

Empty.

No signs of life. All the doors to either side were open, and that struck him as peculiar. Did not some of the whores stay in those rooms at night? Would they leave them open, even if the saloon was one that served breakfast?

He hesitated, not liking the dread growing in his belly. His hand went to his gun, slipped it out of its holster. Then he eased the window up in fractions, making as little noise as possible until he got it wide enough to admit him.

In the hallway, he paused again, listening. No sounds came from below and that puzzled him. Should there not be at least some noise? Voices of the barkeeper or women? No sounds came from any of the rooms ahead, either. It was as if the place had been completely abandoned.

He crept forward, gun ready. Peering into the first room, he found it deserted. The next room proved the same, though he spotted evidence in the form of cigarette stubs littering the floor and empty whiskey bottles on a nightstand that it had been used recently.

A prickle of unease shivered through the hairs on the back of his neck. Something was wrong here. He was now convinced the gang had been here, yet were no longer. In itself that was no surprise, after last night's events. But added to the eerie silence, it set off a warning in his nerves.

In the doorway of the third room, he stopped, ice-water flooding his veins. His dark eyes narrowed as they took in the interior of the room and his hand tightened on the gun handle.

He searched every corner, swept out a palm to make sure the door hit the wall to tell him no one was hiding behind it.

When he was certain nobody living hid in the room, he entered, went to the body tied to the chair near the window. He studied at the body, eyeing the chest where a bullet had punched through bone, and blood had soaked the undershirt. He had never met Trace Cooper but he was certain it was him, and great sorrow filled his heart. Another death for Kemosabe.

"I didn't need him any longer," came a voice behind him, and he realized in his grief he had lost concentration for only a moment, but it was enough. He whirled, met by the *skritch* of hammers being drawn back.

"Drop your gun, Injun," the woman said, her own leveled on him, along with those of two other men beside her.

"Why did you kill this man?" Tonto said, letting the gun slip from his fingers and clatter to the floor.

The woman laughed, an icy sound. "He told me what I wanted to know. Spent half the night gettin' him to squawk, but he did. Dan Reid, the Ranger's nephew. Wish I had time to bring him to the party, but I've got you for that, haven't I, Injun?"

"You are the leader," Tonto said. "I do not know you. Kemosabe would not, either."

"Oh, I'm sure you'll both recognize my name once you hear it. Unfortunately you'll be takin' it to your graves with you."

The dread simmering within the Lone Ranger's mind turned instantly to horror the moment he pushed through the batwings. While he was on the alert, expecting some sort of play on the leader's part when he reached the saloon, nothing could have prepared him for the carnage before his eyes.

"Good God…" he whispered, gloved hand tightening on the ivory-handled .45. Before him lay a sea of bodies—cowboys, bargirls, the barkeep—all sprawled over tables and on the floor, over the counter, riddled with bullet holes. Blood soaked the sawdust and the silence of death hung heavy in the room. The stench of an abattoir soured the air. The sight froze him for one of the few times he could recollect, then he forced himself to move, take the three steps to the barroom proper. With a wave of crashing realization, he knew this is what had resulted from him coming in here last night. It was his fault, in a way, and it would be a burden on his soul until the day he died.

Whoever this gang leader was, she had gone far beyond what Butch Cavendish had ever done. Cavendish was a maniac, but this woman was an inhuman monster. None of these people had stood a chance. The killing was wanton, wholesale.

He forced himself to take steps toward the back staircase, stepping around bodies. He noticed the corpse of the young woman from the alley, Tilly, sprawled half over a table, bloody hand out-stretched, as if for help that never came, eyes still flung wide in terror. He stepped over to her, gently laid a glove hand over her eyes, clos-

114

ing the lids.

"I'm sorry..." he muttered, throat tightening with emotion. Monsters like this woman who led the gang were the reason he existed, hid behind a mask. They seemed legion, unending; the moment one like Cavendish perished another sprang up to take his place, and go beyond their predecessors in terms of cruelty and bloodshed.

He would never be able to wipe the memory of this massacre out of his mind, but it was something he would have to deal with later. Right now, Tonto was here somewhere, likely upstairs, and getting to his friend was his first priority. They could then go back and try questioning the fake marshal for any leads to the identity and whereabouts of the gang leader.

He took the stairs on legs that were less sturdy than he wished, but gathered himself as he reached the top. He paused, listening. No sounds came from the upstairs. Of course, that might not be worrisome; Tonto would make none.

He drifted down the hallway, gun ready, and peered into each room as he passed.

When he came to the third room from the last, he stopped, horror again sweeping through his senses.

It took him only a moment to determine the room was empty, save for the body in the chair. Trace Cooper. The rancher had been shot dead, but a knife protruded from his chest—Tonto's knife.

The knife pinned a note to the dead rancher. The Lone Ranger pulled the knife free, wiped it on the mattress and sheathed it in his boot. He opened the note, read it. It held two words that sent a chill snaking down his spine: Bryant's Gap.

The knife told him they had Tonto and the note told him where. The gang leader held the advantage, had sprung the trap, despite their best efforts at caution.

Whirling, holstering his gun, the Lone Ranger swept out of the room. Three minutes later he threw open the door to the telegraph office, and went to the counter. Spotting the body of the murdered operator, he frowned, went around to the telegraph and began tapping out a message. He had precious little time and he knew it. If Tonto wasn't already dead, he soon would be. But somehow he had to delay, even the odds. He had no doubt facing a whole gang led by this vicious woman would mean both his and Tonto's deaths if he simply charged in unprepared.

Finished sending, he left the office. The message might not help, might not be in time to save Tonto, but he had to try.

He ran back toward the marshal's office. He'd left Silver tethered in an alley two streets over. The heaviness of death dogged him. This gang leader was something inhuman, worse than a rabid animal, with an unquenchable bloodlust. She had to be stopped—even if it meant his own death in the very place he'd lost his brother—Bryant's Gap.

#

Fifteen minutes later the Lone Ranger rode into Bryant's Gap, the ghosts of his past riding in with him. Minutes had dragged as the great white horse beneath him galloped across the rock-strewn hardpack, hoofs kicking up clouds of dust. This time he might not ride out of the small canyon alive. This time he knew the ambush

116

awaited and he would charge straight into it just the same. This time that open sixth grave might truly be eternal home to his bones. There was no other way. If there were even the slightest chance of saving Tonto, even at the sacrifice of his own life, he would take it.

Ahead.

The Lone Ranger's heart stuttered.

A man was staked spread-eagle to the ground, unmoving. Even at the distance he could tell it was the Indian who'd ridden beside him these many years.

"Go, Silver!" He heeled the horse faster, the stallion neighing, hoofs eating ground.

At last he slowed, approaching the figure. His gaze swept out and up, caught the glint of sunlight off rifles on the canyon ridge to his right. Five men, at least, all waiting for him, their weapons trained on the Masked Man.

He reined up, face tight. Without hesitation, he jumped from the saddle, slapping the horse on the rump and sending him charging from the canyon. No need risking the horse's life as well. Silver would be around if he needed him.

He glanced up again; the men hadn't moved. They were waiting, would not fire until the leader said whatever it was she had to say.

He went to Tonto, his heart sinking. Bruises shown livid on the Indian's face, and one eye was swollen closed. Cuts crisscrossed his bare chest and arms. His wrists and ankles hard been tied with rawhide to stakes pounded into the hardpack. Those bonds were tightening with the sun's heat and Tonto's perspiration.

"Kemosabe…" Tonto's voice came out raspy, low.

"Go…I am…already dead…"

The Lone Ranger swallowed hard, shook his head. "Then we die together, faithful friend."

The Ranger started to bend for the knife tucked in his boot, but a shout stopped him.

"Ranger!"

His gaze lifted as he straightened. A man had come from behind a boulder, a man wearing a duster and low-pulled hat, Smith & Wesson in hand.

No, not a man. A woman. Boyish, but still a woman.

"Let him go," the Ranger said. "Kill me."

A laugh sounded from the gang leader and she reached up, whipping her hat from her head and flinging it to the ground. The Ranger did not recognize her features, but it was plain she knew him.

"He's going nowhere, Reid. He'll die first, so you can watch. Then after I kill you I'll be paying that nephew of your'n a visit, thanks to Trace Cooper."

The Ranger's eyes narrowed and anger sizzled through his veins. He had taken a vow to take outlaws alive, if possible, but this woman made him wish he had never made it.

"Who are you?" he asked. "Why have you lured me here?"

"First things, first, Reid. Unbuckle your gunbelt and toss it on the ground. Now!" She switched her aim to the Indian.

He complied, unbuckling the belt and tossing it a handful of feet away.

"I asked you a question," he said, voice hard, colder than he had heard himself since the day he made his pledge for justice in this very canyon years ago.

118

A sound reached his ears, and he almost smiled. It was distant, a slight rumble. He and Tonto might die here today, but this woman was not going kill anyone else ever again.

She gave no indication she heard the sound, her attention locked on him. As she took a stepped forward, her ice-green eyes widened.

"My name's Laura Cavendish, Ranger."

His belly tightened. Cavendish. The name rang in his mind, a death knell. "Butch Cavendish has no relatives."

She uttered a vapid laugh. "I was his wife, one of 'em, at least. I killed the rest, so you might say that makes me exclusive. Even had us a couple young'uns."

"Why? Why lure me here?"

"It's simple. Revenge. I want you to suffer, and I want you dead. He'd still be alive if it weren't for you and that Injun."

"I didn't kill him." He knew it didn't matter. He was stalling, waiting, searching for a way to save Tonto's life, as well as his own.

In the distance the rumble grew louder.

"You were responsible indirectly. You should have died that day with the rest. You're an aberration, a ghost. You'd died Butch would still be alive. I'd still have him. You know what true loneliness is, Masked Man? It's having everything that meant anything to you taken away, leavin' you on this gawdamn dustball thinking about it night after endless night. Those thoughts never stop, Reid. Those nightmares never end."

Behind the mask, the Ranger's eyes hardened. "I know, Cavendish. I've known since the day your husband

119

killed my brother and five other men worth a lot more than you or him. Good men, willing to die for a just cause, not eager to kill for fool's gold."

A dark grin spread across her lips. "Always the moralist, right to the end." The fingers of her free hand went a pocket in her duster, came back out. Something small and shiny glinted in her hand. She tossed it to the Ranger, who caught it.

A copper bullet.

She suddenly raised her gun, prepared to pull the trigger and put a bullet into Tonto's staked form. She wanted him to watch his friend die, suffer a last time before he followed the Indian to the grave.

"Stay in your grave this time, Ranger!" she said.

"Riders!" a shout came suddenly from one of the men on the ridge and Laura Cavendish's head swung.

"What the hell—" she said.

"Rangers," the Masked Man said calmly. "I telegraphed them before I came here. They have long memories for the name Cavendish."

"Gawdammit!" she yelled, head coming back around. She was going to kill Tonto anyway.

He dove, tucked his shoulder as he came down on it and rolled over, coming up next to his gunbelt.

Laura Cavendish saw the danger of him getting to his gun, swung her aim toward him and fired, but it was a hasty shot, poorly aimed. The bullet plowed into the hardpack near his feet.

He grabbed his gun, yanked it free of the holster and fired from a crouch. He was hoping to hit her gunhand. He missed, the shot too difficult from his position.

Gunfire erupted from the ridge. The first shots hit

120

around him, kicking up dust as he sprang up and ran toward the woman, then suddenly switched directions as the riders thundering from the horizon drew closer, loosing their own volley of gunfire.

Laura Cavendish screamed a curse and whirled, running for the trail next to the graves that snaked up to the lefthand ridge. She must have had a horse ready up there, he guessed, was retreating, as much a coward as all outlaw kind, including her dead husband.

He ran after her, gaining ground.

She reached the trail, began ascending, stopping only briefly to fire a shot over her shoulder.

He zigzagged, making himself a difficult target, trying to keep to the shelter of boulders and rock that jutted out from the side of the canyon wall.

The trail grew steeper the farther up they went, narrowing to a precarious degree. He triggered shots, not trying to hit her, merely slow her, despite the urge to end the monster that was Laura Cavendish.

She swung back again, firing over a shoulder. Copper chipped rock from a boulder near which he poised. She kept running while firing, blasting one shot, then another. Around him rock shards lacerated the air and copper slugs ricocheted. He ducked behind boulders, returned fire, silver digging into the ground near her feet. She was moving too fast and erratically to get a proper aim on her gun hand; he might miss and kill her, though it took every ounce of his oath and will power not to do so after the hell she had caused.

Near the top she twisted suddenly, trying to draw a better bead on him, fired.

He dove for cover as again copper spanged from

rock, chipping a piece into stone splinters that stung his face.

Where she stood the trail had become treacherous and her sudden whirl played hell with her balance, the gun's recoil adding to the situation. As she hastily took aim and squeezed the trigger again, the hammer clacked on an empty chamber.

A grim smile came to his lips. Her gun was empty. He stepped from the boulder, began mounting the trail toward her. Still off balance, she screeched and hurled the gun.

He snapped up a forearm, deflecting the weapon. It hurt, but he barely felt it. Only one thing was in his mind: stopping this monster of a woman.

Laura Cavendish tried to flee upward, as he closed the distance between them to a matter of feet. She would not make the top before he overhauled her.

But she miscalculated how close to the edge of the trail she'd come. Her boot skidded on the edge, might have gained enough leverage to propel her forward, but the earth, made brittle by the intense sunlight, gave way.

Her arms windmilled and she plunged downward.

The Ranger lunged, grabbing at one of her arms, but her frantic motion made the grip impossible.

She hurtled from the side of the canyon, a scream trailing after her. A thud came as she slammed into ground below.

He peered over the edge, gaze searching. Her body had hit the side of the empty grave, fallen in. Head lowering, he popped the gate of his .45, extracted the last silver bullet in the chamber, then slapped the gate shut. With a sigh, he tossed the silver bullet into the grave with the body of Laura Cavendish.

She was gone, as was Butch, but the horror and pain their murderous lives had left behind would remain always. The blood-stained memories would not fade, in the mind of the last surviving Ranger and the families of the victims in Coopersville. The Masked Man felt little satisfaction with her death, only grief and the ever-present loneliness that haunted him and Tonto each day of their lives.

Around him gunfire cascaded for dragging moments, but in truth it was over in a very short time. The five outlaws were no match for a dozen Texas Rangers. They fell, bodies riddled with lead.

The Lone Ranger holstered his gun and made his way in slow heart-burdened steps down the trail. If there were any solace in all the death that had occurred in this canyon of Hell, it was that Tonto's life had been spared. He cut the Indian free after he reached the bottom of the trail, then gave a sharp whistle. Silver came galloping at the call. After strapping on his gunbelt, he helped a weakened Tonto into the saddle, then climbed on behind him and took the reins.

One of the Rangers approached the horse, one the Masked Man recognized from a long time ago. He turned his face away, knowing despite the mask he needed to take no further chances of being recognized, even by a lawman.

"We got them all," Captain Striker said, gazing up at the Lone Ranger. "Who's the woman?"

"Their leader. Laura Cavendish."

"Cavendish…" Striker's voice went grim. "There's a name I thought I'd never hear again. When you

123

telegrammed I could hardly believe it."

The Lone Ranger nodded. "You and me both, Captain. I pray the legacy of death will end with her. There's a last one of her gang in the jail in town, masquerading as a marshal…and a lot of bodies in Coopersville that need burying."

"Hell of a thing, isn't it? This place is goddamned cursed."

The Ranger's head lifted, the memory of his brother rising in his mind. "No longer, Captain. No longer—Hi-yo, Silver…Away!"

The great white horse bolted forward, taking the Ranger from the canyon of death, he hoped for the last time.

#

Captain Striker went to the open grave, peered at the body within, then at the name on the marker. His brow furrowed and he looked back to the two figures on horseback growing smaller in the distance.

"I'll be damned," he whispered.

"What was that, Captain?" a younger Ranger said, coming up behind him.

"Fill this grave in, Trendle. Leave that outlaw's body in it. It's more than she deserves."

The younger Ranger nodded, looked to the distance. "Who was that Masked Man, Captain?"

"That, Trendle…that was the closest thing to a legend as you'll ever see. That was the Lone Ranger…"

The End